THERESA T. STARK

TO KILL THE FIRST BORN

FOR LIFE OR DEATH ETERNALLY

ISBN: 978-1-965951-13-2 (sc)
ISBN: 978-1-965951-14-9 (ebk)

Seraphim Global Media LLC
155 Willowbrook Blvd Ste 110
Wayne, NJ 07470
848 800 6538
info@seraphimgml.com

To my daughters, Nyemah, Sia, and Renee, who have really encouraged me to go on and write this book in spite of all odds. To Joan Carroll-Flowers, who, when she heard the title, said, "I know this is from God." And of course, to those in my church who did not know the challenges and disagreements we had were part of my pruning to walk the talk. To my past apostle and co-pastor who helped develop the prophetic side of me and laid hands on me according to the Word. I thank all who have been in my life before and after my salvation, who were in the plan of God to get me, not only where I am today, but also where God wants me to be.

FOREWORD

TO KILL THE FIRSTBORN
(FOR LIFE OR DEATH ETERNALLY)

I have not read a more detailed and Biblically expert book that explains the necessity of receiving the Holy Spirit (with the evidence of speaking in tongues), and the ensuing mag- nitude of understanding the death, burial, and resurrection of Jesus Christ as it directly relates to the believers' personal benefits. These pivotal foundations are set in this text in truth and with personal examples as well as scriptural sup- port that provide an anchor for continual growth. Moreover, Prophet Theresa's unique flow of revelation in this book expounds upon the spiritual reality of the battle between the two nations within man, a tenet not understood, captured, nor taught by many.

As projected in her introduction, the author's intent is that the text of this tome touches the pulse of those who desire to be healed physically, mentally, and emotionally; emphatically, it does so. The content hits the target to inspire complete wholeness for each reader.

Further, captured by the author is the pundit scriptural delivery of why the firstborn must die. Anyone desiring step- by-step clarity of this truth will be thoroughly satisfied while being sub-merged with hope and delivered into a place of security and peace after embracing this section of the book. The same holds true for the chapter "It Is Finished", a section of reading that illuminates truth about thoughts and ques- tions that have rarely been answered in such an authoritative, yet palatable form on the penned page. Chapters following also reflect this ability in the explanations about Paul's teach- ings in Romans and Galatia, and the amplification of the Ten Commandments and more.

Prophet Theresa's panoramic contributions in this book are indisputable scholarly, yet they invite the ordinary stu- dent to read the text and be blessed. The author's personal testimony in "Destiny's Door" is a powerful tool that gently escorts the reader to submit to the entire content of the writ- ten work. The reader mentally, figuratively, and emotionally walks with the author through her experiences, by way of personal pictorial imagery. One feels a confirmation of trans- formation from religion to rela-tionship while reading the "death of the firstborn, Theresa" when she embraces all of the Bible. It is amazing.

Not all books meet the criteria to become generational read-ing, transcending textual gender and age-targeting. To Kill the **FIRSTBORN** meets and exceeds such standards. After becoming a student of this tome an internal beseech- ing will emerge in the reader beckoning and welcoming the author's next book, Vessels of Silver and Gold.

Respectfully, "I AM" Fellowship Ministries Drs.
Michael & Cecilia Jackson, Apostles

ACKNOWLEDGMENTS

This manual was inspired by the Trinity of God: the Father, Son, and Holy Ghost because without them, I would not have been able to see, understand, or even comprehend my healing. Not to mention my relationship with the Lord God as I was then able to understand my privilege to be healed because of the work on the cross through Jesus Christ. The inspiration to write this book was given to me by the Lord. He opened my eyes in 1988 as the Holy Spirit helped me to have enough faith to receive what was already mine through Jesus Christ, my Lord and Savior.

INTRODUCTION

Books are written to help one in business, education, and in the medical field. They can be training for a skill, such as carpeting, painting, and building a building. Some books give step-by-step instructions on how to get rich, be success- ful, cook a dish, or play and sing a song. But this book is about the only book that can help mankind both reach their destination and purpose with full satisfaction. How can I say this? It is because I have read the book called the Bible, and it can bring wisdom, prosperity, wholeness, healing, miracles, acceptance—internally and externally. Guess what? It only takes following directions. It can be hard when you have to let something you had loved and cherished all your days go until you find Jesus. Over the past years, I had disclosure with friends and separation because of death of a loved one. I have experienced direct attacks, both verbally and behind my back— oh yes, from a best friend, a parent, boss, and loved ones—that pierced my heart. But I accepted the Holy Spirit. What I propose to you is by reading this book, you will find, as I have found, the richness of God is simply submitting to God and saying yes and amen. That following Jesus Christ is how to put your stake in the ground for eternal life. You will find that making choices for life is what we do most of the time without thinking. Just do it.

Most of my earlier years, I wondered around in thought, yet it would circle back to God. Being around God-fearing grandparents and my mother kept me out of many things. Although in my youth, without even knowing what I sought were spiritual things, not knowing any difference, I went to haunted houses for fun, played with the Ouija board, seeking things in the spiritual realm. Funny how that desire did not go far. I was steered to seek God and was He real? At twelve years old, I joined church and wanted to be a part of God's heaven. As years passed, I was cautious about things, but never really knew why. My grandmother always sang about going to heaven, which sounded like where I wanted to go. As I got older, got married, and started having kids, my hun- ger for satisfying the Lord became stronger. I pondered, *Is my desire for God a midst, or is He real? Why am I here?* All I could see in the world were turmoils, lies, murder, hate, backbiting, adultery, fornication, and homosexuality.

One day, God called me out by name. I did not know it was God. I heard this voice call my name, "Theresa." Because I was home alone, I ignored it and kept doing my closet. You see, like yourself, I was not taught to listen for God to call me like Samuel the Prophet.

Years later, I attended a women's group meeting to worship God, and bingo, I was introduced to the Almighty God Himself, filled with the Holy Spirit and speaking with tongues. It was not a rit-ual that was performed, just a request in prayer, and Jesus answered.

As I began reading the Bible more, I wanted to expe- rience a closer relationship with Jesus. As I began enjoying the presence of God, no other fulfillment or substitution worked. Later, I had a wilderness experience, a challenge with a deadly disease at that time called "lupus." Watching my body destroying itself was not fun. But my relationship with Jesus pulled me completely through without remission. Still, today, I am healed by His promises in the stripes Jesus took on His body. For me, they were nailed to the cross so I could be healed, was already healed before Lupus, and is still healed today. My internal medicine doctor got saved and told me that he included me in his book.

This book inspired by God's Holy Spirit will explain further why one must accept His Holy Spirit with speaking in tongues and point out more revelation as to why Jesus had to go through the experience of the cross, had to die, and be risen from the dead for us. Otherwise, we would remain trapped in this earthen vessel, living for eternal death from God. Just like God created the earth and the fullness thereof, He created you and me to take dominion over the earthen vessel He sent us also to earth to bring His kingdom here. No matter where we live on earth, He fashioned us to represent Him and to destroy the evil character I created for me. Today, it is the battle between you and yourself.

In the Bible (King James Version), you will find that God exposes to us that we are created with two nations within us. We have to make a choice as to which one we will end up in eternity—the kingdom of God or the world of Satan. Whether you know it or not, our spirit is previously owned by God. It is up to us to willfully choose Jesus Christ and repent, namely stop sinning and live for God. I do not know about you, but I got tired of trying to please man who does not really appreciate what you have done but just tolerate you for their own gain. I found no benefits accepting things of the world. It just slowly gets eviler and self-centered— placing me toward loneliness. It will become me, myself, and I for my eternal death from God. All the money in the world will not buy your ticket to eternal life. But surrendering to God, accepting Jesus Christ as Lord and Savior, and being filled with the Holy Ghost will help me destroy the life of death, killing the firstborn. What is the firstborn? It is clearly stated in the Bible and is identified in this book.

This book is to anyone who has searched for the full- ness of God and want all that He has planned for them and nothing more. To those that want to be healed in any capac- ity, physically or mentally, I pray as you read this book, you will understand more clearly the privilege and righteousness the Lord Jesus has provided for you to walk in wholeness with divine health. You are a joint heir in the kingdom of the Almighty God. That healing is part of your inheritance as a son of God. Jesus accomplished and supplied all that is ever needed for man, standing in proxy for us to gain back what Adam lost in the beginning. The debt is now fulfilled in Him. The atonement and propitiation were made once and for all, forever and ever through Jesus's death on the cross. But He lives and is the victor who overcame, by His shed blood and the thirty-nine stripes bore on His body, clearing the channel for us to also become the victor with Him.

> For all the promises of God in Him are yes, and
> in Him Amen, to the glory of God through us.
> (2 Cor. 1:20, NKJV)

May the grace of our Father and the anointing of His Holy Spirit open the eyes of all who are inspired to read this book and who seek wholeness in the Lord, spirit, soul, and body, where no compromise is allowed.

The Spirit of the Lord spoke these words to Me. Those that want more of Me will come and be prepared for My return. Nevertheless, the time is now to write all I have shared with you for them to know. Some still need milk, some are ready for the meat of the word and others just the strength of this book will move them out of one season to another to a greater walk in life. This will strengthen their walk with Me and sharpen their tongues to be Holy as I am Holy when they understand what it means to kill the first born.

"Only as high as I can reach can I grow, only as far as I seek can I go, Only as deep as I look can I see, Only as much as I dream can I be"[1] (Karen Raven).

---

1   "Karen Raven Quotes," Quoteopia, accessed January 30, 2018, https://www.quotes.net/quote/16853.

WHY SHOULD THE FIRSTBORN DIE?

Cause me to hear thy lovingkindness in the morning; for in thee do I trust; cause me to know the way wherein I should walk; for I lift up my soul unto thee.

> Teach me to do thy will; for thou art my God: thy spirit is good; lead me into the land of uprightness.

> —Psalm 143:8, 10 (KJV)

There is something about telling someone that you want to give them your soul, even if it is God. Most of the time, we as humans hold onto our souls because it is our mind will and emotions that contain the real us. You see, that is what God wants from us—our will. Your soul was with Him before you were born. What are you saying? The Word of God says in the book of Psalms 139:13–15 (KJV):

> For thou has possessed my reins; thou hast covered me in my mother's womb. I will praise thee; for

> I am fearfully and wonderfully made; marvelous are thy works; and that my soul knoweth right well. My substance was not hid from thee, when I was made in secret, and curiously wrought in the lowest parts of the earth.

> Your eyes saw me when I was inside the womb. All the days ordained for me were recorded in your scroll before one of them came into existence. (Ps. 139:16, NET)

Believers, I cannot express it enough, that being filled with the Holy Ghost (Spirit) is our escape from hell, freedom to live again, and eternal peace. It enables one to break free from confinement of being locked in the level of the earth life only and not enter the kingdom of God. If one does not fol- low the directions demonstrated by Jesus Christ, as a follower of the Lord, we are then fitting into the mold of the seventy who were disciples. They saw this journey as a Christian too hard, too restricting, less controlling, and will not allow me to be myself. Well, you are correct. It is hard when you have protected your abilities to sustain in the refinement of man. When some have only accepted God the Father and/or Jesus, His Son, and will not accept the Holy Spirit, who is part of the Trinity of God, just as Jesus is part of God. You only have two-thirds of God and want to also be your own god. Who needs the Holy Spirit anyway? Jesus demonstrated at the River Jordan that we need the Holy Spirit. At Gethsemane when He prayed, it was the power of the Holy Spirit that He surrendered His will to God. On the cross, Jesus entrusted His soul to God. What makes us feel that we can do less? Jesus, our Lord, is the best teacher and the ultimate demon- strator, and He said,

> And he that taketh not his cross, and fol- loweth After me is not worthy of me. He that findeth his life shall lose it; and he that loseth his life for my sake shall find it. (Matt. 10:38–39, KJV)

And he who does not take up his cross and follow Me [cleave steadfastly to Me conforming wholly to My example in liv- ing and, if need be, in dying also] is not worthy of me Whoever finds his [lower] life will lose it [the higher life] and who- ever loses his [lower] life on My account will find it [the higher life]. (Matt. 10:38–39, AMP)

We as followers of Christ must also accept the Holy Spirit with the evidence of speaking in tongues. Accepting God and the Lord Jesus is good. But as a follower of Him, as your spir- itual advisor, He said that He would pray to the Father, and He will give you another Comforter, that He may stay with you forever. Even the Spirit of truth, whom the world cannot receive, because it seeth him not, neither knoweth him. But you know him for he dwelleth with you and shall be in you (John 14:16–17, KJV), and I will send you assistance to help you be successful while living on earth. That He would not leave us comfortless and called Him the Comforter. He, the Comforter, is the only one that can allow you to enter the kingdom of God. We as humans are made to carry the Holy Spirit as Adam and Jesus did and ultimately all His disciples. So how is giving my soul so significant? What is the big deal? I am who I am, and having control to what I feel is import- ant. I have had some bad times and some good times. But I made the decisions that I thought were right. And I say to you, so did I. Everyone on earth has done the same thing prior to being filled with the Holy Spirit of God Almighty. As most of us have read the Word of God a number of times, even then it may have been a textbook reading, using only the Webster Dictionary as an assis- tance to define biblical words when the Word is either written by Hebrew or Greek men and trans- lated by an Englishman? Well, sometimes using Webster helps with the English interpretation. Then there is also the Hebrew and Greek Study Bible, as well as the Strong's Concordance. But the ultimate understanding comes from the Holy Spirit who wrote the Bible through men. He is the one who gave me this insight, and now I am sharing it with you.

At first, I was apprehensive, but then once I realize who was speaking to me, I received and was able to see through my spiritual eyes what the Holy Spirit was saying and ulti- mately showed me in the Word. Prior to reading the Word of God, I always pray this prayer from the scriptures.

> Father, Open thou mine eyes, that I may behold wondrous things out of thy law. (Ps. 119:18)

> For Howbeit when he, the Spirit of truth is come, he will guide you (me) into all truth; for he shall not speak of himself; but whatsoever, he shall hear that shall he speak and he will show you (me) things to come. He shall glorify me; for he shall receive of mine, and shall show it unto you. All things that the Father hath are mine; therefore, said I, that he shall take of mine and shall shew it unto you. (John 16:13–15, KJV)

So as I am reading the Word of God, I expect that the Holy Spirit will reveal the truth of what was written to help me under-stand who and what I should be as a follower, a repre- sentative, and demonstrator of what Jesus Christ of Nazareth said I would do. After all, the Holy Spirit is the true author that allowed man to write what He spoke in his thoughts, documenting God's Word to His kingdom people. With that being said, the following informa-tion will help you to under- stand why the firstborn must die spir-itually to relinquish all you have learned from Satan's kingdom. To learn God's way a new and how to survive through your five senses and intellect. But to also embellish the foundation, princi-ples, statutes, and precepts of God's kingdom. Thereby, learning to be led by the Holy Spirit of God. Submission to the Holy Spirit is the key. Submission is an attitude, not action.

The following are the chapters and verses the Holy Ghost opened my eyes to see how significant it is to be filled with the

Holy Spirit of God and why the firstborn must die. Not only be filled with the Holy Spirit but to have a bet- ter understanding as to why the firstborn of an individual must die. We have to die spiritually because our very soul, character, disposition, while living in our flesh hinders our Christian rank.

Remember this lyrics, "Onward Christian soldier! / Marching as to war / With the Cross of Jesus / going on before." Although this song was before man really understood the writer, this writer was given insight as to what the body of Christ's position would entail. Because Jesus still intercedes and stands in the gap for His followers, His work on the cross lives today and will be active tomorrow and forever.

As I was studying the Bible during my recovery, the Holy Spirit further defined areas that pointed out the direction for us to follow after leaving heaven. Because our earthen vessels were created for us to come through with God, we must not adopt man's way of living—constantly seeking man's wisdom, the desires of the world, and think that we accomplished anything on our own. When we come into the world, because of Adam's fall, we automatically adopt Adam's nature of sin before becom- ing a living soul. We function as an individual without God, open for either the infilling of the Holy Spirit or entrapped by the world system of Satan. We constantly have to read the Word of God with the Holy Spirit, our helper, to renew our minds and redirect our life in the earth to glorify God.

When we are reconnected to the Father through the Holy Spirit, He will help us to sustain our position and plan God originally created for us. In His creating us, He placed His plan within, and with His Spirit, we will be able to ful- fill our God-ordained purpose. We then become diplomats of the kingdom of God, not Satan's domain. Accomplishing things or ruling people who are uncomplimentary to our life has hindered the body of Christ. It has striped us of the power God wants us to reveal and demonstrate with Him, for His glory. We need to relearn how to be holy again. Remember, we were holy before we came to earth (Ps. 139:13–15).

I prayed that He will do the same for you as you read the following five sections of the Bible (Basic Instructions Before Leaving Earth). This will bring clarity as to why the firstborn must die.

Let's start with Genesis 25:21–23 (KJV):

> Isaac entreated the Lord for his wife, because she was barren; and the Lord was entreated of him, and Rebekah his wife conceived. And the children struggled together within her; and she said, if it be so why am I like this? And she went to inquire of the Lord. And the Lord said unto her, two nations are in thy womb, and two manners of peo- ple shall be separated from thy bowels and the one people shall be stronger than the other people; and the elder shall serve the younger. And when her days to be deliv- ered were fulfilled, behold, there were twins in her womb…

Unlike animals, we are created in God's image for Him and by Him. Unfortunately, He gave us the ability to make our own decisions called a free will. Having the will to go with Jesus or stay in sin against God. We have the option to be a part of one of two nations within us. When we get born again in the Holy Spirit we become eligible to actively participate in the nation of the spirit realm. Our body will spiritually separate and the new born you will begin growing within. We can choose to hang with the first-born from our earthly parents or go with the second birth in the Spirit of God's kingdom. Unlike animals, we can choose to magnify Lord Jesus who gives the Holy Spirit to us as a gift and be in the Kingdom of God. Or we can choose to continue in the nation of the devil pleasing our flesh. It is that simple.

SECOND SCRIPTURE

> When the time came for Rebekah to give birth there were twins in her womb. The first came

out reddish all over, like a hairy garment, so they named Esau. When his brother came out with his hand clutch- ing Esau's heel, they named him Jacob. When the boys grew up, Esau became a skilled hunter a man of the open field, but Jacob was an even-tempered man, living in tents. Now Jacob cooked some stew, and when Esau came in from the open fields, he was famished. So Esau said to Jacob, Feed me some of the red stuff—yes, this red stuff-because I'm starving! But Jacob replied, First sell me your birthright. "Look", said Esau "I'm about to die! What use is the birthright to me?" But Jacob said "Swear an oath to me now." So Esau swore an oath to him and sold his Birthright to Jacob. Then Jacob gave Esau some bread and lentil stew; Esau ate and drank, then got up and went out. So Esau despised his Birthright. (Gen. 25:24-34, NET)

Although this example is not apples to apples the prin- ciple is the same. God wants us to be born again both in water and in the spirit in order to enter the kingdom of God. We as humans have the same option in life. We can choose to stay as a Worldly person in Satan's domain or relin- quish our earthly firstborn body to be born again with the Holy Spirt having the second birth and be in the kingdom of God. God blesses the spirit-filled, born again saint who has allowed their souls to be rescued back to himself. Let's look closer at how God has emphasized the necessity of one to be reconciled back to him.

THIRD SCRIPTURE

When Joseph brought his children to his father Isreal (Jacob) for blessing from God.

And Joseph took them both, Ephraim in his right hand toward Isreal's left hand and

Manasseh in his left hand toward Israel's right hand, and brought them near unto him. And Israel stretched out his right hand, and laid it upon Ephraim's head, who was the younger and his left hand upon Manasseh's head guiding his hand wittingly, for Manesseh was the first born... And when Joseph saw that his father laid his right hand upon the head of Ephraim, it displeased him; and he held up his father's right hand to remove it from Ephraim head unto Manesseth head. And Joseph said unto his father, not so, my father; for this is the firstborn; put thy right hand upon his head. And the father refused, and said, I know it, my son, I know it, he also shall become a people, and he also shall be great; but truly his younger brother shall be greater, and his seed shall become a multitude of nations... God make thee as Ephraim and as Manasseh; and he set Ephraim before Manasseh the older. (Gen. 48:13–20, KJV)

Now before I lose you, I want you to ask the Holy Spirit to reveal this truth to you as only He can. We as God's creation was made in His image. We have a body, a soul, and a spirit. We are the only creation that God made in His image. When we are born, we come equipped to receive the Holy Spirit of God. Adam had the Spirit of God up until he sinned. His covering and direct connection to God ended, and Adam lived a life of body and flesh. His soul became earthly and had to work for everything. Jesus came into the earth as we did through the womb of a woman completely created to carry the Holy Spirit.

He [Jesus] delivered us from the power of darkness and transferred us to the Kingdom of the Son he loves, in whom we have redemption,

> the forgiveness of sins. He is the image of the invisible God, the firstborn over all creation, for all things in heaven and on earth were cre- ated by him—all things, whether visible or invisible, whether thrones or domin- ions, whether principalities or powers All things were created through him and for Him. (Col. 1:15–16, NET)

Jesus received the Holy Spirit at the River Jordan. The same potential is within all human beings. Our capability to walk in the Spirit lies in the core of our body in a dormant state until Jesus sends the Holy Spirit (the Comforter) to be activated within us in conjunction with the Holy Spirit of God. You have to make the choice. To represent the Kingdom of God or the domain of Satan. That is it.

The Holy Spirit ignites your spirit and ushers you into the kingdom of God, initiating the born again experience, except this time you are born in the spirit. As a newborn kingdom person, the younger you has to learn how to walk and live in the spirit. Once born again, the Holy Spirit will now begin transforming your lifestyle and help you become a kingdom member of the body of Christ.

Once you have accepted the Holy Spirit, you imme- diately become an overcomer, redeemed of God, set apart from your flesh, and begin the real life in the kingdom of God. You're born again. Once you receive the Holy Ghost and begin desiring to read the Word (the Bible), you will then begin changing the way you do things, think, talk, and walk. Your body, also known as the firstborn (you), and the name is _ will begin literally "dying to self." Once we receive the activation of the true Holy Spirit, we are a Son of God, a Daughter of Zion, a King, a Priest, a representative of the kingdom of God. We are successful because Jesus did all the work when He completed the work of the cross. When He received the sour wine vinegar on the cross He said, *"It is finished,"* and He bowed His head and gave up the ghost (His spirit) (John 19:30).

So I ask the question: What is taking you so long to be a prime example of the kingdom of God and a living sacri- fice, holy and acceptable unto God? What is taking you so long? Do you enjoy the world so much more than being a representative of God? Do you really know who you are and whom you should be serving? The King of kings and Lord of lords—the Great I Am. What an honor and privilege we are given, and it is all free. Just live as the Holy Spirit leads you. I know it is hard to follow Him. It was for me at first, but I had to decide for me, and I made an eternal decision. Because living for the world's recognition, ambition, pride, and haughtiness characteristic slowly shapes our personality to the father of this world, and we become less useful for God. Before you know it, you compromise and find excuses about being too spiritual and deceivably think that you have to have a balance. Well, that has been the direction we have taken, and the world still sees the church as another orga- nization and not where God is. Compromising has caused the church assembly of God to be less and less attractive or desired. An individual's ultimate decision should be: "To live is Christ; to die is gain."

> So then, brothers and sisters, we are under obligation, not to the flesh, to live according to the flesh (for if you live according to the flesh, you will die), but if by the Spirit you put to death the deeds of the body you will live. For all who are led by the Spirit of God are the sons of God. For you do not receive the spirit of slavery leading again to fear, but you received the Spirit of adoption, by whom we cry, "Abba, Father." The Spirit him- self bears witness to our spirit that we are God's children. (Rom. 8:12–16, NET)

The fourth witness to kill the firstborn (our earthly compromising self-satisfying self without the true Holy Spirit) is to become a believable witness for the kingdom of God. By the way, the devil will still try to impersonate God to win the souls of man until the end of time when he himself is thrown into the lake of fire. He is not going to stop because he wants you and me with him. That is why you need the Holy Spirit of the living God to live a Christian life and go back to heaven.

Christ not only demonstrated the infilling of the Holy Spirit, but He also showed us that we are to submit our will to the Father and do the things of the kingdom of God like he did at Gethsemane. The Lord was going to pray to the Father and verify his next steps. Because Jesus prayed every evening to get the Father's advice on His next move, Jesus knew what is to happen next but wanted to see if there is a change. (Remember, Jesus was still in an earthen vessel, and the flesh wanted to opt out of this next move. Yet, Jesus knew that this move was His entire purpose for coming to the earth. He knew that there will be a spiritual battle regarding the two nations of mankind, His Spirit [the kingdom of God versus the kingdom of dark- ness.]) This time Jesus's next move was for your soul and mine. So Jesus requested from His closest disciples to undergird him in prayer. (Is that going to be you for His second coming? He is no respecter of person.) Jew or Gentile, it does not matter (Acts 10:34–35, KJV); when Peter was told by God that He will use anyone that fears Him and worketh righteousness will be accepted with him, Jesus knows who is praying, reading the Bible, and are willing to follow him without question. Trust me. He knows who you are. Yet the disciples were willing as most Christians are. Jesus already knew their weaknesses. He uses them to demonstrate what you and I will do today. When Jesus left them to pray and inquire of God, the Bible says they had heavy eyes and was found sleeping. After a second return, they were found sleeping again and not able to stay awake and pray.

> Then he came and found them sleep- ing, and said to Peter, "Simon are you sleeping? Couldn't you stay awake for one hour? Stay awake and pray that you will not fall into temptation. The spirit is willing, but the flesh is weak. (Mark 14:37b–38, NET)

Jesus left and prayed the same thing of God to take this cup (his next direction) away from Him.

> And he said, Abba, Father, all things are possible unto thee; take away this cup from me; nevertheless, not what I will but thou wilt. (Mark 14:36, KJV)

> He came a third time and said to them. "Are you still sleeping and resting? Enough of that! The hour has come, Look, the Son of Man is betrayed into the hands of sinners. Get up, let us go. My betrayer is approaching!" (Mark 14:41–42, NET)

In this passage, Jesus revealed to us that we cannot stand without the Holy Spirit. The Lord has given us the authority to pray with the Holy Spirit and power. Praying is not just in your own language and always for your own personal needs. Most, if not all, of the Christians prayer should be through the Holy Spirit and the Word of God because we tend to only pray for our needs or gain. Not praying God's Word or for His Kingdom to come and His will be done on earth and in us.

Why don't we allow the Holy Spirit to reveal to us what we should be doing? Is it the fear of not controlling your actions? Not getting the recognition or acknowledgment of what you did? When are we going to submit to God's plan? Being hum- ble and meek. Listen to the Holy Spirit; He will guide you into all truth for He shall not speak of Himself but whatsoever He hears *from God* that shall he speak (John 16:13–15).

Fifth and final examples in the Bible regarding the sec- ond birth "to kill the firstborn" within us and graduating into what God wants us to become is in Exodus 13:15:

> And it came to pass, when Pharaoh would hardly let us go, that the Lord slew all the firstborn in the land of Egypt, both the firstborn of man, and the firstborn of beast: therefore I sacrifice to the Lord all that openeth the matrix,

being males; but all the firstborn of my children
I redeem.

So how is one redeemed? The Word tells us that we are redeemed in several passages, all the following scriptures are from the KJV Bible:

> Let the redeemed of the Lord say *so*, whom he hath redeemed from the hand of the enemy. (Ps. 107:2)

> Christ hath redeemed us from the curse of the law, being made a curse for us: for it is written, Cursed *is* every one that hangeth on a tree. (Gal. 3:13)

> And they sung a new song, saying, Thou art worthy to take the book, and to open the seals thereof: for thou wast slain, and hast redeemed us to God by thy blood out of every kindred, and tongue, and people, and nation; and has made us unto our God kings and priests; and we shall reign on the earth. (Rev. 5:9)

> These are they which were not defiled with women; for they are virgins. These are they which follow the Lamb whith- ersoever he goeth. These were redeemed from among men, *being* the firstfruits unto God and to the Lamb. (Rev. 14:4)

Submission to the Holy Spirit is the key. Remember that submitting is an attitude, not an action. Submission to the Holy spirit protects you from the enemy. We have to learn how to submit as in the book of James 4:10: "Humble yourselves in the sight of the Lord and he shall lift you up." As we are promoted to the kingdom of God by Jesus Christ, we can pray and know that we are granted kingdom asylum and diplomatic immunity from evil that seeks to impress and entrap you. "Rescue me from mine enemy for I hide myself in you" (Ps. 143:8, 10, KJV). My place in Christ eliminates my place in the world, for I no longer walk after the flesh but in the Spirit. My mind is renewed day by day.

IT IS FINISHED

> I have glorified You down here on the earth by completing the work that you gave Me to do.
>
> —John 17:4 (AMP)

> When Jesus had received the sour wine. He said, "It is finished!" And He bowed His head and gave up His spirit.
>
> —John 19:30 (AMP)

Many times, I would think about these three words: "It is finished." What did Jesus mean when He said "It is finished"? Many teachings and preachings about these three words have been ministered to open our eyes as to why the Lord was saying those three words. I myself had often wondered about why did the Lord have to say "It is finished" while on the cross. Other people would scream and cry because they were hurt or in pain, asking for help. But Jesus said, "It is finished." Once a year, recognition is given to the crucifixion of Jesus Christ. Many church services identify His life coming into the world as a child and ending his life beaten by man and hung on a cross. While on earth, Jesus loved, taught, and corrected man's thoughts and conditions. He delivered man from demons, healed the sick, recover sight to the blind, and did signs and wonders. He did miracles, such as changing water to wine, when all they did was fill huge waterpots with plain water. Another time, he had to restore an ear that was cut off a soldier's face by Peter, one of the disciples. The sol- dier was stunned when he felt his ear being cut off, seeing it fall to the ground in one moment, and in the next moment, Jesus picked it up, placing it on his head and restoring it as if it never happened. Jesus, also being the teacher, was demonstrating to his followers what they could do, yet He told them,

> Verily, verily, I say unto you, He that believeth
> on me, the works that I do shall he do also; and
> greater works than these shall he do; because I
> go unto my Father. (John 14:12, KJV)

In other words, we, as true followers of Christ, will do things even greater than Him. Yet centuries have gone by, very little signs and wonders or miracles have happened by a few pastors and has occurred mainly over the last few decades. Not much has happened that the unsaved wants to be a Christian. The understanding of why Jesus would say "It is finished" while hanging on the cross is still a little puzzling so one gets saved. What else was He referring to? What was ending or had to be completed?

On Resurrection Sunday, Easter Sunday for others, Jesus's death, burial, and resurrection are shared in numerous ways. In reading the Bible, King James Version (KJV), you will read about his life. Jesus rose from death after being dead for three days in a tomb. He later reappears to the believers, assuring them that He is healed and alive. But was that it?

I read the Word, and I have sought the Lord asking the Holy Spirit: "To open my spiritual eyes so that I may behold the wondrous things out of Your Word" (Ps. 119:18, AMP). When the Holy Spirit answered, He made those three words so simple and perfectly clear. We must understand that the first and foremost reason Jesus Christ went to the cross was for everyone to be saved. "For God so loved the world that he gave his one and only son, that whoever believes in him shall not perish but have eternal life (John 3:16, NIV). But was that it?

Jesus Christ went through a horrendous death for us. It must be more than that. The Holy Spirit revealed that it was more than that; it is deeper than that. Then what else was He referring to? Besides salvation for us He died so we could not only know the Father but also have a relationship with him. It is not an option, neither is it an opinion. Jesus's death on the cross made the way (path) back to God, the Father. You see, the first man created by God in His own image was Adam (Gen 1:27, KJV), who was made from the dust of the ground, and God breathed in to his nostrils the breath of life (His Holy Spirit); and man became a living soul (Gen. 2:8, KJV) God was able to communicate directly with Adam because God's Spirit was in him, completing the image of God on earth. Therefore, it made it easy for Adam to hear God. Well, Adam fell from the presence of God in the garden of Eden when he ate the fruit given to him by his wife, Eve. The fruit she gave Adam was from the tree of the knowledge of good and evil which was in the midst of the garden.

Now, for those who do not know in Genesis 2:16–18, God commanded Adam that he could eat of every tree in the garden of Eden, but of the tree of the knowledge of good and evil, he should not eat for when he does, he will die. When Adam ate the fruit given to him by Eve that was from the tree of the knowledge of good and evil, he disobeyed God's command not to eat from that tree. For in the day that he ate from that tree, he shall surely die. What God was referring to is that He had sanctified Adam to be holy with His Holy Spirit and to represent the kingdom of God in power and strength. By eating from the tree of knowledge of good and evil and when it gets in the body of man, it will cause one to become independent and steer away from God, for it imparts evil. Holiness and evil cannot merge or be in the same place. The presence of God (the Holy Spirit) left his body because Adam sinned. He did not do what God commanded and ate fruit from the forbidden tree. God's holy presence will not abide with sin. Adam then became spiritually dead, not physically dead, although he continued to live for 930 years. Now, Adam's thoughts are human decisions generated from his soul, mind, and emotions as a natural man. He is now without God's Holy Spirit guiding him. Adam now had a sinful nature. God's Spirit could not be in Adam as before. God is Holy and Adam chose to follow after the flesh and was thrown out of the Garden of Eden before he would attempt to eat from the Tree of Life.

At that time there were no laws for correction, no redemption to help Adam get back to right standing with God. Hence, the need for Jesus Christ. Now, all mankind affiliated with the kingdom of God is born through the lin- eage of Adam. Because he ate from the tree of the knowledge of good and evil, we are born with a sinful nature without the Spirit of God. Adam, being the first man created in the image of God, made a decision that affected the whole human race, also known as Homo sapiens, which are extant. Anyone born after the fall of Adam is born without the Holy Spirit. We are created as the highest level of God's creation to reveal his image. Our desire without God's spirit is exactly what Adam did. He was influenced by Satan to satisfy himself. In this case, it was his woman he wanted to satisfy. Not realizing that his thoughts changed from obeying God, that's how subtle Satan still comes after mankind because he was right there with Eve when the serpent was speaking with her. When she gave him the fruit in his hand, he ate the fruit to satisfy her. Even though God had told him specifically not to eat from that tree, he knew what he was doing. He satisfied his will, not God's will. Satan influenced Adam by using the woman to get to Adam the authority set by God to take dominion over all. Adam should have taken *authority*, telling Eve that God said that they should not eat from that tree and throw it away.

Our desire is to please ourselves when we are not spiritually connected to God because our body and soul are after the soulful nature of Adam. Adam, being formed from the dirt of the earth, was initially connected to the earth's characteris- tics. He would have no desire to please God. But when God breathed into Adam's nostrils the breath of life, he became a living soul filled with the Holy Spirit. As I mentioned before, all human beings are the highest quality in the creations of God. We are created in His image—with a body, a soul, and a spirit. We are created by God to reunite with Him and carry His Holy Spirit. Unlike other creations on earth—such as animals (fish)—birds are only a body with a soul. Plants, trees, vegetables, and so forth only have a living body as long as they are connected to the earth in soil or water.

The sinful nature caused by Adam eating the fruit from the tree of the knowledge of good and evil turned man into operating in worldly ways of doing, feeling, and thinking to satisfy himself. The problem is that this type of mind-set/ nature separates man from God's tenderness and His tangi- ble love. For this very reason, God sent His only Son, Jesus Christ, to save us and to complete the only path to connect us back with God. The Bible says, "For God so greatly loved and dearly prized the world that He (even) gave up His only begotten (unique) Son, so that whoever believes in (trusts in, clings to, relies on) Him shall not perish (come to destruc- tion, be lost) but have eternal (everlasting) life" (John 3:16, AMP).

Jesus Christ, as the perfect (substitute, sin offering) to die on the cross for you and for me, He said in John 14:6 (KJV), "I am the way, the truth, and the life: no man cometh unto the Father, but by Me."

We must realize that God is real, and He has thoughts, feelings, power, and pure love. He is pure in thought, intent, and motive. He is for us. If God is for you, who can be against you? No one. He really loves us and wants us to come back to him once we physically die. Your spirit leaves the body here on earth. As a follower of Jesus Christ, our spirits will leave our bodies and go to join God's kingdom in paradise (heaven), not the kingdom of Satan. As a faithful believer of Christ, you will have the honor of going to heaven. Anything else is a straight-out lie, rejecting Him. This is another reason Jesus went to the cross and said before dying, "Then Jesus, calling out with a loud voice, said, 'Father, into your hands I commit my spirit! And after he said this he breathed his last'" (Luke 23:46, NET). He was assuring to us that as a persistent fol- lower of Christ, God will receive our spirit when we die. He wants to be up close and personal daily. He wants to have a direct unhindered relationship with you and His Holy Spirit. Another reason "It is finished" is because Jesus is the Truth. "And ye shall know the truth, and the truth shall make you free" (John 8:32, KJV). There is only one true Truth. Jesus said that he is the truth in response to His disciple Thomas, "I am the way, I am the truth and I am the life. No one comes to the Father except through me (John 14:6, NET).

Even God's Word declares that God is Light, and in Him there is no darkness (deception or lies). When a person has the truth opened to them, then they can say the Truth has been revealed. True revelation can only come through those who have a rela- tionship with God through Jesus Christ. Some call it "intuition," defined as a thing that one knows or considers likely from instinc- tive feeling, rather than con- scious reasoning. Some even say it's a hunch feeling that they have, impression or a suspicion as defined by Wikipedia. The Truth (Jesus) will open new insights, wisdom, and revela- tions about life, self, and others around you, even the way you perceive. Your thoughts and ways will change because the touch of the Creator changes all who choose Him. This will happen because as a born-again vessel, you are being transformed into His likeness. God gives us the ability to rec- ognize and under- stand what is missing in our lives or where we personally fall short representing His Kingdom. He never condemns as He reveals to us our earthly, carnal ways. He helps us to see our needs and how we need His help changing our attitudes, pride, haughtiness, jeal- ousy and our character as we read through His word. Without the living bible and the Holy Spirit we would not be able to make it in this world. Let alone properly represent the kingdom of God.

Jesus forgave us for all we have done, are currently doing and will potentially do in the future. It does not mean we sin on purpose and expect God to forgive us from a contin- ued willful sin. It does mean we forgive others and ourselves from hurt, lies, deliberate offenses, repent, turning away from repetitive sinning. We must eliminate the sin because you willfully sinned you can choose to willfully stop. There are times when you may need prayer to be delivered from strongholds, such as anger, lying, fighting, hatred, and bit- terness. Strongholds are dominating thought patterns that keep repeating themselves over and over in your mind. It is also defined in *Merriam-Webster's Collegiate Dictionary* as a fortified place, a place of security or survival, a place domi- nated by a particular group or marked by a partic- ular charac- teristic—as a strongman, one who leads or controls by force of will and character or by military methods.

They can be ignited by association of someone or things that happened in the past. Instead of turning the other cheek and forgiving them, one tends to hold onto the situation in their mind, even to the extent of not wanting to be around that person(s). Once it is held in their heart and mind, they cannot seem to release that incident, even if they tried. More churches should teach about deliverance from hurts, trauma, unexpected death of a loved one, consistent raging or on-oc- casion anger, and little lie that one may feel it did not hurt anyone. Think about it, small things can grow if feed every now and then.

If that is your situation and where you assemble does not offer teaching on kingdom living and deliverance, pray about where you are because Jesus taught his disciples to deliver so one can live. He told them to bind that strongman first to release the captive and be released from its hold. For freedom, Christ has set us free. Stand firm then, and do not be subject again to the yoke of slavery (Gal 5:1 NET). A strongman or stronghold is any mindset that rejects truth and holds a person from truly walking in the kingdom of God.

There are churches that teach their members about being delivered to help them grow in the spirit of God and not fulfill the lust of flesh. Lust of the flesh are worldly desires that is against the commandments and the holiness of God Almighty until one accepts Jesus Christ as their Savior and is born again; they cannot even think of forgiving an individual(s), praying with another Christian of faith, exposing the issue and helping one to be delivered by openly forgiving and denouncing that burden from their thoughts. A few churches that teach deliverance are Bible Way Church of God and Christ in Cincinnati, Ohio, if you are in that area; Crusaders Church in Chicago, All Nations Worship Assembly also in Chicago, or Christian International in Versailles, Indiana— to name a few.

Depending on the struggle getting loosed from that sin, you may have to get help from a known Christian minis- ter that oper- ates in deliverance, like John Eckhart or Ryan LeStrange. But at the same time, you still have to make a decision and want to renounce the demonic influence out of you. The Bible will assist us with the knowledge and wis- dom on how to make any change as an ambassador for the Kingdom of God. An ambassador is an accredited diplomat sent by a country as its official representative. A born again, Holy Ghost-filled Christian, with a repented heart as a fol- lower of Jesus Christ, fits that description. When Jesus died on the cross and rose from the dead, He passed the authority to His followers to truly represent the kingdom of God.

> He said unto them (the disciples) "Go into all the world, and preach the gospel to the whole creation. He who believes and is baptized will be saved, but he who disbelieves will be condemned." (Mark 16:15–16, WEB)

It is that simple. Especially when using the words spo- ken by Jesus Christ himself.

Thirdly, Jesus closed the door on death, hell, and the grave for those of us who choose Him as their Lord and Savior. As a spirit-filled believer, we do not have to ever expe- rience spiritual death from God as Jesus did on the cross. Jesus, the Lamb of God, sacrificed for you and for me, taking all of our sin so we can return to God and receive the Holy Spirit.

Fourthly, He also closed the door on the carnal mind.

> Because the carnal mind is enmity against God;
> for it is not subject to the law of God, neither
> indeed can be. (Rom 8:7, KJV)

Another translation:

> Because the outlook of the flesh is hostile to
> God, for it does not submit to the law of God,
> nor is it able to do so. (Rom. 8:7, NET)

As our carnal thinking is revealed, while reading the Bible, we begin to stop our carnal ways. We renew our minds and change our ways. In understanding the bible and the character of Jesus, our leader, we begin to recognize that we have been tricked into ungodly ways. What does carnal mean? As define by the Interlineal Bible (Hebrew and Greek Lexicon)[2] one definition is "Sarx" 4561:

> 4. the flesh, denotes mere human nature, the
> earthly nature of man apart from divine influence,
> and therefore prone to sin and opposed to God.

The animal nature with cravings, which incite to sin (Roman 8:7–8 KJV), tells us that our minds without the Holy Spirit is sinful and enmity (animosity, hatred) before God. This pertains to the characterization done by your soul. It creates your passion and appetites, gluttony, sensuality; not spiritual, merely human, temporal with worldly desires. We have been living below the Kingdom of God's standards that we once knew. Jesus sealed the opportunity for us to not only reclaim the presence of the Holy Spirit to live in us again as it was with Adam before he ate the fruit. Adam had the priv- ilege of communicating directly with God. No call waiting, answering machine to leave a message, or being placed on hold. But Jesus recuperated access to the kingdom of

---

2   Interlinear Bible keyed to the Hebrew and Greek text using the *Strong's Concordance*.

God for all believers of Him. Jesus did the supreme work and was honored by God with the victory for all of us who choose Jesus.

The fifth major reason is to stop religion as the scribes and Pharisees. Making God unreachable; having to go through man to get to God. Religion has composed their own methods of leading man for them and directing them astray with burdens too hard to bear, and the Pharisees did not do it themselves. Here is an example of the Lord chasing the religious leaders in Luke 11:46 and 52 (KJV).

> And he said, Woe unto you also ye law- yers! For ye lade men with burdens griev- ous to be borne, and ye yourselves touch not the burdens with one of your fingers. Woe unto you, lawyers! For ye have taken away the key of knowledge Ye entered not in yourselves, and them that were enter- ing in ye hindered.

In the past and in some churches today, people are not given the true Word of God. They are not being taught by the spirit of the Bible, but laws that even the Lord challenged them. Religion divides, separates, and twists the Word of God for the comfort of man's flesh—such as creating another type of belief outside of the Word of God. Restricting and personally selecting who can be a leader for their church with false qualifications for leadership (a friend, celebrity, associ- ate). Not knowing their walk with God by their fruit. When the Word of God says he chooses who will lead His people by His spirit. "For without the presence of God, teaching and preaching to mankind, while directing them to grow in Christ, they will stumble and fall, remaining as infants needing milk," says Paul in his return visit to the church in Corinthians. They were not matured from past teachings and still in need of repeated instructions. The members were not taking dominion over the area leading others to Christ.

> I fed you milk, not solid food, for you were not yet ready. In fact, you are still not ready. (1 Cor. 3:2 NET)

Therefore, the current state of the church at large is still in this state, or the church would be recognized as the place to be and the way to live for the kingdom of God.

Still another reason is that we take dominion over the earth. God did not create us to populate hell but to repre- sent His kingdom. As representatives of God's kingdom, we are to only represent Jesus and allow the Holy Spirit to flow through us. Spreading the gospel of Jesus Christ for others to be saved. Not only be saved, but be filled with the Holy Spirit of God. Just as Adam was in the beginning. That's why Jesus could say, "It is finished."

Thank You, Jesus, for doing everything needed so I could come back to God. You did it all and paid it all will- fully just for me. We are free, for whom the Son sets free is free indeed (John 8:36, NKJV). I do not have to go to hell because as one preacher Eve Hill once said, "There is no backdoor in hell." Once you are in hell, you are eternally separated from God.

For those of you who have not accepted Jesus Christ of Nazareth or if you have and have fallen away for any reason, know that the work of the cross still restores anyone today. If you have not received Jesus as your Lord and Savior or need to be reconciled back to God because you were deceived by the devil, then let's pray right now.

READ OUT LOUD

Father, I have not seen this truth before regarding the cross. Help my unbelief or doubt. I have sinned and did not take the work of the cross seriously. I repent of all the sins I did to anyone and to myself. I ask You to forgive me and to wash me with the blood of Jesus. I believe in Jesus Christ, Your Son. You said in Your word that if I confess with my mouth and believe in my heart that Jesus died, was buried and rose again, I would be saved. Come into my heart and fill me with the Holy Spirit who will help me to be right in Your sight. Lord, help me to do what is right and be faithful today. In Jesus's name, I pray. Amen.

Now tell a friend, neighbor or family member that you have received Jesus Christ as your Lord and Savior. And that I am glad about it. The angels in heaven are rejoicing because you have made Jesus Christ your Lord and Savior. (Now hold your head up high.) This is also a confession with your mouth and for your hearing while declaring before the heavens.

If you are not going to a church, ask Jesus where to go. Get a King James Version of the Bible. It is the original Bible translated from Hebrew and Greek language by Englishman King James inspired by the Holy Spirit of God. It was pub- lished in 1611 and copyrighted by Thomas Nelson Publishers 1976. In this version, there are symbols and italic words to help bring clarity to the meaning of the Word so you can better relate to the original English language. It also has the words of Jesus in the color of red, distinguishing when the Lord Jesus was speaking. Because the Bible is living, it can and will define itself with the Holy Spirit, the original writer. The first four books of the New Testament known as the four Gospels read them first: Matthew, Mark, Luke, and John. These books will help you to know Jesus and enhance your relationship with the Father.

The Lord desires that we rest in Him and abide in Him (John 15:4, KJV). While we are an extension of the body of Christ, our portion of spreading the Gospel for salvation is the same for all. It does not matter if you are an apos- tle, prophet, pastor, teacher, evangelist, administrator, pres- ident, king, prince, chief executive officer, director, mayor, city manager, council person, mother, father, or just a sister or brother, to name a few. Stop feeding your mind the past lifestyle. Let the Holy Spirit renew your mind. In order to make the change you must read the Word of God with the Spirit of God.

CHRISTIANITY? NOT WHAT I THOUGHT

"Do not be conformed to this present world, but be transformed by the renewing of your mind, so that you may test and approve what is the will of God—what is good and well-pleasing and perfect. For by grace given to me I say to every one of you not to think more highly of yourself than you ought to think, but to think with sober discernment, as God has distributed to each of you a measure of faith."

—Romans 12: 1–2 (NET)

Being a Christian requires one to stay focus, it is not easy. It is not a one-two-three formula or a pattern man would like to choose. You must allow yourself to make mistakes and surrender to the Holy Spirit to begin growing in the things of God that will guide you into all truth. Remember that He is the creator of all mankind. It requires more than one can comprehend. Because we have embraced the world system and built our lives around what man approves/says is right, we doubt, feel insecure, and have very little confidence in anything that we cannot see, feel, touch, hear, or smell. As a new born-again Christian, we jump into Christianity with both feet and no boundaries. When we read and study the Word of God, we learn that being a Christian means that we will eventually change our character, the way we communicate to others, as well as the choices we make become bibli- cally sound. We learn that one needs to become more and more like Jesus as He demonstrated so well when teaching the disciples throughout the gospels.

You know, many of us have our own systematical way of doing and learning things. As a new Christian, "We Fall Down, But We Get Up" (a song written by Gospel minister and singer, Pastor Donnie McClurkin). The greatest chal- lenge we have as a believer is to reveal His Son in us (Gal. 1:16a KJV), yet it is through our tri- als and tribulations that we begin to make that wonderful change and learn Jesus's ways. As we learn the Basic Instructions Before Leaving Earth (BIBLE) and take it to heart, it becomes easier to go through our test, trials, and tribulations. The Bible is a testament, a legal document from God. It is sent to establish the forma- tion of the Kingdom of God in the earth which is us, the earthen vessel. As we learn to become as He is, that is holy. Let me say this: there are hills and valleys, there are ways of being perfected to reveal the image of Jesus Christ, His Son, that we as human beings cannot conceive. While learning to be a Christian as a new and some old believers, we some- times think that it will be a piece of cake. We memorize or read a few scriptures, and that is the extent of our reading or knowing the truth or even understanding God. What some believers did understand is then summarized as just being good, not breaking the Ten Commandments.

You know, "Thou shall have no other gods before me; remember the Sabbath day to keep it holy, thou shall not kill, thou shall not steal, thou shall not bare false witness against thy neigh- bor, honour thy father and thy mother; that thy days may be long upon the land which the Lord thy God giveth thee" (all scriptures in Exodus 20).

Most of us perceive that everything that is going on in our lives as good, good enough, "I am good," near perfect, etc.

I did everything I thought was good, keeping the Ten Commandments as I judged others that did not. I kept on lifting myself up on how I don't do those things. As I kept reading the Word of God, I found that I was falling short. I was not a nice person. I used profanity like a sailor. I was stubborn as a bull. Very aggressive and only submitted to anyone other than my parents for gain. I was controlling and wanted my way or there was no way. Whatever it took for favor outside of sex I would do. I would support anyone for friendship, that had an advantage or had an opportunity for financial gain. But for some reason believe it or not I feared God and my parents. I did not want a person to fail. It did not matter who they were I wanted to help them and myself be successful.

As I was reading the Word daily, it was transforming my mind and renewing a right spirit within me. "And Be not conformed to this world but be you transformed by the renewing of your mind, that you may prove what is that good, and acceptable, and perfect, will of God" (Rom. 12:2, NKJV). I began having more patience with people, my chil- dren, my husband. In my reading, I also found this scrip- ture that says: "Knowing this, that the trying of your faith worketh patience. But let patience have her perfect work, that ye may be perfect and entire, wanting nothing" (James 1:3–4, KJV). While sin has its consequences, the Lord had warned us that as His follower we would suffer persecution. But according to the word of God,

> Blessed are you, when men shall revile you, and persecute you, and shall say all manner of evil against you falsely, for my sake. (Matt. 5:11 KJV)

> or

> Blessed (happy to be envied, and spiri- tually prosperous with life-joy and sat- isfaction in God's favor and salvation, regardless of your

outward conditions) are you when people revile
you and per- secute you and say all kinds of
evil things against you falsely on My account.
(Matt. 5:11 AMP)

Jesus, our Lord and Savior, has demonstrated many times how we are to walk in this earth, triumphing over every trail and tribulation with victory every time. There are many accounts when the Lord was showing us how to handle our trails through patience. Three major trials and tribula- tions were demonstrated by Jesus after He was filled with the Holy Spirit at the River Jordan. He was immediately led up of the Spirit into the wilderness to be tempted of the devil. The Lord had patience working in Him as the Son of Man filled with the Holy Spirit when He was directly tempted by Satan, questioning the Lord's ability as a man to stand on the principals of the kingdom of God. The devil himself used the three major areas that he uses to distract or remove man from becoming an over-comer and is still true today. The three areas that men (women) still struggles with and is still working today are these:

> For all that is in the world, the lust of the flesh,
> and the lust of the eyes, and the pride of life, is
> not of the Father, but is of the world. (1 John
> 2:16, KJV)

Case and point. After Jesus had fasted and *prayed* for forty days and forty nights, He became hungry. (Notice the tempter came after the fasting and *praying* was over.) Satan comes to Him, challenging Jesus at the end of the fast with trial one—*lust of the flesh*—and tells Jesus, "If thou be the Son of God, command that these stones be made bread." Jesus, in his wisdom, says, "It is written, man shall not live by bread alone, but *by* every Word that proceeds out of the mouth of God" (Matt. 4:4, NKJV; italics added). Satan knew that if Jesus would eat that bread after not eating for 40 days the body is not ready to digest heavy starches or foods. One must rebuild their eating habit gradually. It has been medically proven that forty days is the longest one can fast without eating and the absolute longest a person can fast and live because after 40 days the body begins to eat its muscles. Bread is not the right type of food to eat after a 40 day fast. Your stomach has shrunk and bread would swell up and potentially bust the stomach.[3] Why didn't he offer a roasted chicken or fish? He wanted to kill Jesus. Additionally, Satan referring to the stone to be made bread he was trying to get Jesus to eliminate the stone/rock the Chief Cornerstone the foundation used to build the kingdom of God. Satan wanted Jesus to start doing things that did not benefit the Kingdom of God. Jesus knew that He is the only foundation for the Kingdom of God to be manifested in the earth. Later in the gospel of John, Jesus said: From this moment on, everything in this world is about to change, for the ruler of this dark world will be overthrown.

And I will do this when I am lifted up off the ground and when I draw the hearts of people to gather them to me (John 12:31–32, TPT). Jesus was referring to Him being lifted up on the cross and saying "It is Finished."

Fasting is one of the things Jesus demonstrated for His believers to do. Fasting is also not a means for loosing weight but to make one more capable of flowing in the Spirit and not fulfill the lust of the flesh. It is also demonstrated throughout the Word as a means of seeking closeness to God for direc- tion and strength as well as increasing their spiritual relation- ship with God. (This does not mean to read the Word and not eat to keep the earthen vessel. However, He does mean to live as a true Christian. Reading the Word of God daily will keep us with power and strength in our spiritual connec- tion as we walk in the spirit.) It does mean that the Word of God *will keep* you kingdom minded *and able* to be about the Father's business. Fasting is part of what a follower of Jesus will do. It helps to decrease the flesh which the body wants to do more for yourself, like overeating, fornication, lying, adul- tery, stealing,

---

3   Dr Myles Monroe research and teaching on Understanding the Power of Prayer and Fasting. As well as my own personal experience with prayer and fasting.

drugs, cursing, backbiting, and drinking alco- hol—to name a few. But it will increase the capacity of your spiritual quality. You will be taking control of your body and soul with its constant demand to be self-satisfied at any cost.

The devil's next area of tempting Jesus was *"the lust of the eyes."* "Then the devil taketh him up into the holy city, and setteth him on a pinnacle of the temple" (Matt. 4:5, KJV). A pinnacle in Greek is "Pterugion," meaning a wing, any pointed extremity of the top of the temple in Jerusalem; *Pterux* is the root word, meaning a wing of birds. Satan who also knows the Bible and remembers he is the tempter of the flesh. He was referring to the Bible, where it says in Psalm 17:8 (KJV), "Keep me as the apple of the eye, hide me under the shadow of thy wings." The devil wanted Jesus to foolishly make God protect him as he would be committing suicide in the flesh by jumping of the temple and arrogantly saying, "I will show you who I am. I have bodyguards (angels) that will protect me no matter what I do." And saith unto him. If thou be the Son of God, cast thyself down for it is written He shall give his angels charge concerning thee: and in their hands, they shall bear thee up, lest at any time thou dash thy foot against a stone. He was paraphrasing the word to tempt Jesus, as he did with Eve in the garden of Eden.

> But the Word says: For he shall give his angels charge over thee to keep thee in all thy ways. They shall bear thee up in their hands, lest thou dash thy foot against a stone. (Ps. 91:11–12, KJV)

The devil began showing Jesus the richness of the world which God originally owned. Remember, Adam lost man's authority by disobeying God. The devil wanted Jesus to assume the human position with self-satisfaction and go after the things of the world (the lust of the eyes: greed, power, fleshly fulfillment, coveting what others have, addictions, etc.). "Jesus said to him, 'It is written again, You shall not tempt the Lord your God" (Matt. 4:7, NKJV). Some of us do try and challenge God saying, "If,"

"When," or request some sort of compromising action with God because of our insecurity like I did in my trial with zealous belief instead of faith. I said, "I will not take the medication because you have healed me." I called myself, taking authority by declaring, "After all, I have to believe that the beatings Jesus took on the cross, at least one is for me to be healed. Why do I need the medicine? Jesus took all sicknesses and diseases on his body, and one of them represented lupus for me. So I will not take my medication." (I will share later on how that panned out.) Well, since the lust of the eyes did not work, Satan tried Jesus for the third and final trial as he does with any man, and this time, it is in *"the pride of life"* by telling Jesus what he could give Him if He would bow down and worship him.

> Again the devil taketh him up into an exceeding high mountain and sheweth him all the kingdoms of this world, and the glory of them; and he said unto him, all these things will I give to thee, if thou will fall down and worship me. (Matt. 4:8–9 KJV)

Of course, Jesus, who is the Word, knew how to respond and said, "Away with you, satan! For it is written, 'You shall worship the Lord your God, and Him only you shall serve'" (Matt. 4:10, NKJV). We must be mindful of replacing God with the things of this world to substitute Him like Israel did with the golden molten calf approved by Aaron who was next in charge after Moses.

The people noticed that Moses was taking a little longer in the mountain with God than usual, and they began to get anxious, *gathering around Aaron. Let me paraphrase their expressions*: "Why isn't Moses back yet, he is taking too long, for all we know Moses could be dead. We want to worship God too. We need to see *our* God." Aaron agreed with them and had them to bring him the golden earrings from the *ears of the wives, sons, and daughters,* and he, with an engraving tool, made a molten calf. They claimed it to be their gods, and Aaron proclaimed the next day to have a feast to the Lord. *While they were celebrating this visual god, the Lord Himself was speaking to Moses and said:*

> They have turned aside quickly out of the way that I commanded them.
>
> They have made for themselves a golden calf and have worshiped it and sacrificed to it and said, "These are your gods, O Israel, who brought you up out of the land of Egypt!" (Exod. 32:8, ESV)

Was it jealousy arising with the leaders because they wanted to be with God too? Substituting God is not what the Bible says. We are to go to Him and inquire what to do and say. Jesus laid the path for us to overcome any trial or tribulation. What has been our excuse? We were created in the image of God. The ability to know right from wrong is instilled in human beings naturally, but we are not a god. Our mind is created to know naturally when something is not right. We see things that just are not right from the training of our parents or guardian, combined with our own cul- tured belief. Some say they had a hunch; others say, "I had a gut feeling." Even though it is wrong, we rather suffer the consequences and enjoy pleasure for a season. We tend to override our own values and just do it anyway, even knowing it is wrong according to our own ethical beliefs. The Bible says it this way.

> Choosing rather to suffer affliction with the people of God, than to enjoy the pleasures of sin for a season. (Heb. 11:25, KJV)

Sin can only bring pleasure for a season. That pleasure outside of God's will always demands a repeat to keep one in a state of regrets. Yet it becomes easier when repeated because the flesh is enjoying it. Then later, when doing it, there is no remorse at all. One becomes insensitive. The Bible calls it a reprobate mind.

> They profess that they know God; but in
> works they deny him, being abominable,
> and disobedient, and unto every good work
> reprobate. (Titus 1:16, KJV)

> And just as they did not see fit to acknowledge
> God, God gave them over to a depraved mind,
> to do what should not be done. (Rom. 1:28,
> NET)

> And even as they did not like to retain God
> in their knowledge, God gave them over to a
> reprobate mind, to do those things which are
> not convenient; (Rom. 1:28, KJV)

In the Strong's dictionary's New Testament section, Greek Lexical Aids #96, it is called *adokimos*. A sinner who is not of the elect and is unapproved, unworthy. In other defi- nitions from Google Dictionary/Wikipedia (in Calvinism), it means predestined to damnation.

Well, Jesus died and rose again so we can repent, ask God to forgive us, and helps us to recover our relationship with him and to not do it again. It will take the Holy Spirit and your will to help you to willfully sustain from continuing that sin again. He will help you. He will not force you to stop.

You have to want to stop. God will not control or manipulate you to quit. Remember, it's your will that is needed.

As followers of Christ, we should observe how Jesus handled any challenge. It is written:

> If any of you lack wisdom, let him ask of God,
> that giveth to all men liberally, and upbraideth
> not; and it shall be given him. (James 1:5, KJV)

Why did those leaders need to substitute God with an image? Was it "the lust of the eyes," "the pride of life," or "the lust of the flesh"?

The character of Adam without the Holy Spirit con- tinues to be how mankind functions overall today. We aim to please others or ourselves. Most of the time we want our own satisfaction no matter how it affects others. So long as we are content, recognized by our friends or bosses and ful- filling their thoughts we become of like minds. Still pleasing man and not the Almighty God. Once we accept Christ, and really read the bible, our self-taught per- sonality seems irrev- erent. You find that becoming a Christian is not what you thought. Thus, the three areas we do not really pay attention to are the very areas we love to submit to. Because it is our will and pleasure. Your soul does not want to give up what you have created to be you all these years. So, you continue to be what you have nurtured to be you. Typically, it is influ- enced by your family traits, or the surroundings in society.

The *pride of life* is what you believe you have accom- plished because of your confidence in all your previous suc- cesses. Nothing wrong with that except we tend to leave God out and give a soft mentioning to no credit to Him, such as riches, fame, land, house, and even a job or business. For example: the Emmys and Oscars awards, athletic victories, completing a construction project with a ribbon-cutting ceremony, or simply having a business successful for twenty- five-plus years. When you are publicly acknowledged and are called to accept the award or recognition. God's praises are given to your personal accomplishments. Your family support, all the groups that made the award possible—from directors, sup- porting actors, musicians, maybe a grandparent—but it is all how you persevered and did it on your own. When you get the award, all, if not most, of the gratefulness is to mankind and those you worked with and lifted you up. Most awardees tend to identify to others how they accomplished the great- ness so others can recog- nize all that they have done.

When one gets world recognition, they feel that they accom- plished to be the best. They identify what they did, how they obtained ownership, and now they have ten additional stores, businesses, restaurants, construction companies all over the world. Some acknowledge God and their spouses but tend to forget any testimonies for Christ and how He made a way because they did it all. No room for God, Jesus, or the Holy Spirit. They forget witnessing, primarily because they are ashamed of mentioning God. The devil placed in the govern- ment a "church and state policy" to stop witnessing for Christ. To the point where some are not living as a representative of the kingdom of God outside of the church building but want personal recognition for their own kingdom of this world.

Can a person look at you and know God is with you? From your family or coworkers, cashier at the stores, or when you are pumping gas? Then we have work to do in repenting and staying clean in our hearts before God every minute of our life. We only fool ourselves if we say we are a Christian and continue to sin a little. Who are we fooling? Surely not God. When you look in the mirror, do you see a servant of the Most High God, or do you see yourself made in the image of pride?

Secondly, is the *lust of the flesh* today no different than the days of Moses? People still overeat, satisfying the belly, have addictions to drugs, alcohol, fornication, adultery, homosexuality—anything that replaces God and your time with Him. We know one or two scriptures and think that will keep us holy. Well, you are wrong. If you are not giving the Word of God, the Bible, more of your time, then you still cherish your idols that rule you, replacing God.

Thirdly, the *lust of the eyes* is clearly what you see and want to have in your possession. It travels from the eyes to your heart, appealing to you, and the desire increases. Satisfaction only arrives when you have conquered, depending upon the type of the desire one tends to arrange for public recognition. Such as more than one expensive car or home, another male or female that appeals to you sexually, married or not. More gold, silver, acres of land and buildings. Just materialistic as one can be to show your abilities and skills to obtain any- thing. *I can possess what I want when I want it. This proves I can do anything and accomplish greatness not realizing or inten- tionally crushing others along the way. After all, I got everything on my own. I can get it and rule over it.* These thoughts are just like in the beginning with Eve, when Satan lured her to see the fruit as an opportunity to be like or greater than God. All she had to do was just eat it and give it to Adam. Then he can see also. Besides, it will make one wise like God. Just possess it, and you will be like God, knowing everything.

These three things are not the characteristics of a Christian. They are not given to us from God. Remember:

> Because all that is in the world (the desire of the flesh and the desire of the eyes and the arrogance produced by material pos- sessions) is not from the Father, but is from the world. And the world is passing away with all its desires but the person who does the will of God remains for- ever. (1 John 2:16–17, NET)

As we study the bible, we find that as a Christian we have to change what we believed to be a Christian. If we truthfully look at ourselves we find that being a Christian or what we perceived it to be "it is not what we thought". We need the characteristics and passion of Christ not mankind. As true believers in Christ, we must change everything about us. As we begin to understand what Jesus was teaching, we find that Christianity is the opposite of anything the world system has acknowledged to be the alternative for living.

TO PERSONALLY KNOW GOD

> And these signs shall follow them that believe; In my name shall they cast out devils; they shall speak with new tongues; They shall take up serpents; and if they drink any deadly thing, it shall not hurt them; they shall lay hands on the sick, and they shall recover.
>
> —Mark 16:17–18 (KJV)

Another interpretation says it this way:

> These signs will accompany those who believe: In my name they will drive out demons; they will speak in new languages; they will pick up snakes with their hands, and whatever poison they drink will not harm them; they will place their hands on the sick and they will be well.
>
> —Mark 16:17–18 (NET)

Every one of us have at least one weakness. No matter how hard we try, the weakness always wins out. We surrender to that habit and lose control. Well, when you are not making time daily, preferably start of your day with the Lord, reading and praying, to get help with that weakness. It becomes a habit that soon becomes the norm.

So, can praying first thing in the morning become a habit? Yes. You will find that when you pray before the Lord and wait for the answer, things fall in place. The more you read the scrip- tures, it becomes easier to know the will of God concerning you. When you pray, have faith to believe that you are talking with Him. Be still like you do when you are speaking with any- one and wait for Him to answer. God is a living God and does like to talk with His people. The Holy Spirit will help you to hear God, like Adam did before he sinned. God is no respecter of persons. He does commu- nicate. He will give an answer to your request, questions regarding the day or family. When you meet someone for the first time and want to have a relation- ship, you study them. You learn what they like or dislike; what they eat or not; the colors they like; and their habits, good or bad. Well, the same holds true with understanding God and learning Him. In His Word, God tells us as an individual:

> Study to show thyself approved unto God, a workman that needeth not to be ashamed, rightly dividing the word of truth. But shun profane and vain bab- blings: For they will increase unto more ungodliness. (2 Tim. 2:15–17, KJV)

Another translation:

> Make every effort to present yourself before God as a proven worker who does not need to be ashamed, teaching the message of the truth accurately. But avoid profane chatter, because those occupied with it will stray further and further into ungodliness, and their message will spread its infection like gangrene. (2 Tim. 2:15–17, NET)

God wants His people to study His Word and to know Him—what He likes, dislikes, and even hates. Studying the Bible with the Holy Spirit will help you remember His Word. When you are praying God's Word and learn of Him, His will becomes your will as well. By praying God's Words then, He becomes responsible to respond. But when you pray your own words, it is not His responsibility because it has no merit for the kingdom of God. The joy is that He will bring satis- faction, completeness, or resolution to the situation. If you can learn to be still for two minutes or less after spending time with Him, He will answer.

You can develop your relationship with God, doing His plans for you. Or we can find ourselves doing chores that have no eternal benefit but satisfies our earthly needs. Just like our purpose to do exercise or walking for our health rou- tinely. You may start, but being consistent will bring victory.

We have internal thoughts and reasonings. Some of us have full conversations with ourselves. Instead of talking to God, most of the time we talk at God, not with Him, and do not stop to listen. How would you like someone talking to you, and you never get a word in? I have found that a one- way conversation can be frustrating, discouraging, and it is an incomplete dialogue unless one is declaring and decreeing the Word of God. That is God's will, not ours; we are bab- bling. When you read the Bible, you will know what He said. He will hasten to perfume His words, not yours.

> Then said the LORD to me, Thou hast well seen: for I will hasten my word to perform it. (Jer. 1:12, KJV)

I selected this scripture because it directly addresses when, what, why, and how God Himself responded to answer- ing mankind. The word "performs" in Hebrew is called *asah*, which means to do, make, wrought, deal, commit, offer, exe- cute, keep, shew, prepare, work, do so, to attend to, put in order, get, dress, maker, and maintain. God needs no one to do His work. He is a God of His Word and His Word alone. Our words generated by our own fleshly state does not obli- gate God to respond. He does not own what we want Him to own, but He will back up His Word. When you pray with God wanting an answer, He responds because of His Word. He responds to a pure heart, cleansed from sin and submitted to Him not Satan. Although you are working toward a clean heart, He will answer, especially when you respect Him and His Word. Be honest with Him for He already knows what you will do. Remember, He created you. (I will discuss Him knowing you later.) His response becomes quicker as we willfully repent and turn from our wicked ways; we become submitted to him alone. And again, yes, He answers. As a sheep of His pasture, He will respond.

So let's take God out of the box and allow Him to be who He is in you—the Almighty Sovereign God. There can be a change with how He wants you to flow. So relax and be open to the Holy Spirit and take God out of the box "you created for Him." We have to admit that we ourselves create our own cocoon and think that we can keep someone else from getting ahead when we actually are holding ourselves hostage and in some cases blame the Lord. Remember we have to repent and turn away. No one can do it for us. Our will has to be truly wanting to please God not man. God knows all so we cannot play games with Him. Humble your- self under the mighty hand of God. He will forgive you if you confess with your mouth.

The Bible verses put it this way:

> I am so ashamed, I feel such pain and anguish within me, I can't get away from the sting of my sin, against you Lord! Everything I did, I did right in front of you. For you saw it all. Against you, and you above all, have I sinned. Everything you say to me is infallibly true, and your judgement conquers me. (Ps. 51:3–4, TPT)

Another translation in KJV says:

> For I acknowledge my transgressions: and my sin is ever before me. Against thee, thee only,

have I sinned and done this evil in thy sight:
that thou may be Justified when thou speakest,
and be clear when thou judgest.

Be a vessel that says "yes" to the Holy Spirit without question
and have faith in God. Consider what I say, and the Lord will give
you understanding in all things. The Word of God tells us that Jesus
said that those that follow Him will do greater things than He did.
So when sinners or fallen saints come to church with the thought
that "this is not what I thought" and they will have their needs met
and actually see the Kingdom of God in operation; then, we have
won them for God. They leave satisfied and healed both mentally
and physically that their hearts will begin seeking more of Jesus.
Spend more time with the Holy Spirit so we do not offend sinners
or fallen saints. Just keep in mind that the Word says,

> And whosoever shall offend one of [these] little
> ones that believe in me, it is better for him that
> a millstone were hanged about his neck, and he
> were cast into the sea. who cause a stumbling
> block to them. (Mark 9:42, KJV)

There must be the love of God in every believer, no matter
what creed or race, gender or age. Once saved, we experience the
true love of God in our heart. If we take the next step and receive
the Holy Spirit with the evidence of speaking with tongues, we have
accepted all the Lord had demonstrated at the River Jordan when
He was baptized both with water and spirit. Jesus, as a man was able
to go successfully through trials and tribulations, surrendered to the
Holy Spirit. Now that is the truth, and the Word of God says,

> And ye shall know the truth, and the truth shall
> make you free. (John 8:32, KJV)

> If the Son therefore shall make you free, ye
> shall be free indeed. (John 8:38, KJV)

When the Lord Jesus answered Nicodemus, one of the Pharisees, a ruler of the Jews, He said, "Except a man be born again he cannot see the kingdom of God." Like any other human would think, he would have to be reborn through his mother's womb. As a natural man and our earthly knowledge about birth, we would believe that a man can only be born again through a female, but in the Word of God, it says,

> Nicodemus saith unto him, How can a man be born when he is old? can he enter the second time into his mother's womb, and be born? Jesus answered,

> Verily, verily, I say unto thee, Except a man be born of water and [of] the Spirit, he cannot enter into the king- dom of God. That which is born of the flesh is flesh, and that which is born of the Spirit is spirit. Marvel not that I said unto thee, Ye must be born again. (John 3:4–7, KJV)

For those of us who have experienced the infilling of the Holy Spirit sent by Jesus, we then understand what He meant when Jesus said that He must be born again to enter the kingdom of God.

> For the kingdom of God is not meat and drink; but righteousness, and peace, and joy in the Holy Ghost. (Rom. 14:17, KJV)

> For the kingdom of God [is] not in word, (idle talk) but in power. (1 Cor. 4:20, KJV)

> There hath no temptation taken you but such as is common to man: but God [is] faithful, who will not suffer you to be tempted above that ye are able; but will with the temptation also make a way to escape, that ye may be able to bear [it]. (1 Cor. 10:13, KJV)

Another translation says it this way:

> No trail has overtaken you that is not faced by others. And God is faithful: He will not let you be tried beyond what you are able to bear, but with the trial will also provide a way out so that you may be able to endure it. (1 Cor. 10:13, NET)

No one has a unique situation, no one. Somewhere in this world, there are other people going through the same thing. But what is unique for us is that those who have accepted Jesus Christ as Lord and been filled with the Holy Spirit has an option. We, by faith, can close our minds to the chatter discussions of the devil speaking in the battleground of our minds and can counteract the thoughts by asking Jesus, "Lord what is my next step?" Jesus said,

> So I say unto you, Ask, and keep on ask- ing and it shall be given to you; seek and keep on seeking and you will find; knock and keep on knocking and the door shall be opened to you. For everyone who ask and keep on asking receives and the one who seeks and keep on seeking finds, and to him who knocks and keeps on knock- ing the door shall be open. (Luke 11:9– 10, AMP)

But what has happened is the enemy has given the wrong information to us and says if you ask more than once, you have no faith or it does not take all that. But when you are learning to walk by faith as you know, repetitions help to change the thoughts and to focus on what to do next.

As we study the word of God, it replaces our thoughts. We begin to stop what we called good and see that it was lined up with this world. We were not really helping others to get saved into the Kingdom of God. But only pleasing ourselves. In reading the bible I also found that if I was not leaning on the Holy Spirit for direc- tion, I was useless in the Kingdom of God. So, with the help of the

Holy Spirit I read the scriptures daily which changed my mind and attitude. When I needed to share with someone about the Lord, the Holy Spirit would bring the scriptures to my thoughts for that person to hear from God. As I kept reading the bible I remained in the vine. The vine Is Jesus Christ and He said,

> Therefore, we are buried with him by baptism into death; that like as Christ was raised up from the dead by the glory of the Father, even so we also should walk in the newness of life. Knowing this, that our old man is crucified with him, that the body of sin might be destroyed, that henceforth we should not serve sin. For he that is dead is freed from sin. (Rom. 6:4, 6–7, KJV)

NET translation says:

> Therefore, we have been buried with him through baptism into death, in order that just as Christ was raised from the dead through the glory of the Father, so we too may live a new life. We know that our old man was crucified with him so that the body of sin would no longer domi- nate us, so that we would no longer be enslaved to sin. (For someone who has died has been freed from sin.)

Control is a human weakness that is in our lives, based upon our experiences and learnings from our family, friends, and others that we regard and respect. We weed out and maintained some of those characteristics. But when the Holy Spirit of the living God's presence is in you and you willingly submit to His leading the weakness of, the worldly control will decrease to nothing. You will have the peace and joy that passes all understanding because you are free. The Word of God will set you free, and we know it is Jesus Christ, our Lord and Savior.

DESTINY'S DOOR THE HOLY SPIRIT

And when you heard the word of truth (the gospel of your salvation) when you believed in Christ you were marked with the seal of the promised Holy Spirit, who is the down payment of our inheritance, until the redemption of God's own possession, to the praise of his glory.

—Ephesians 1:13 (NET)

A certain man among the Pharisees named Nicodemus, a ruler (a leader, an authority) among the Jews, came to Jesus at night and said to Him, Rabbi, we know and are certain that You have come from God (as) a teacher; for no one can do these signs (these wonders, these miracles—and produce the proofs) that you do unless God is with him. Jesus answered him, I assure you most sol- emnly I tell you that unless a person is born again (anew, from above), he

> can- not ever see (know, be acquainted with,
> and experience) the kingdom of God. (John
> 3:1–4, AMP)

Jesus, knowing that some needed additional information, further explained to Nicodemus in John 3:5 (AMP). He said, "I assure you, most solemnly I tell you, unless a man is born of water and (even) the Spirit, he cannot (ever) enter the kingdom of God."

Well, here is part of the problem. Every individual in the congregation or assembly is not born of the Holy Spirit. Some have pretended to be filled by the Holy Spirit and their life style reflects that of the unsaved, with no change in their habits or discussions. Pleasing God or even talking about Jesus is not on their agenda at any time. Instead, pleasing man is more important. Why do you say that? If one never truly repented turning away from their sin and surrendered to God. Discussing things about the Lord will never be a topic or expression exhortation thanking God or witnessing about Jesus salvation for them. Church assembling to them is merely a social gathering. Some still are doing what they did before they accepted Jesus Christ. Still doing what they did before they got saved. The body of Christ is not all born of the Holy Spirit.

While I was living with my parents, my dad was in the Army. Whenever we went to church overseas, it was to attend the church that was on the base—Lutheran, Catholic, or Presbyterian. This went on for six years of my life while liv- ing in Karlsruhe and Heidelberg, Germany. While overseas at the age of twelve, I accepted the Lord Jesus and joined, by letter, the Saint Paul African Methodist Episcopal Church in Cincinnati, Ohio (a.k.a. St. Paul AME Church). This was the church that my father's mother attended whom I loved and lived with in my early life. I wanted to be associated with the church that she was a member because she would always sing songs from Mahalia Jackson like, "I'm gonna walk, I'm gonna walk all over God's heaven, he-e-evin." All I knew at that time was that I wanted to walk all over

God's heaven, so I wanted to be saved and be with Jesus who lives in heaven.

When my dad was stationed in the USA, we attended either a Methodist church, which was his upbringing, or Baptist church, which was my mother's side of the family. I grew up as a teenager in the mid to late '60s; I did not hear anything about the Holy Spirit, and just on certain holidays did I even hear about Jesus much later years. I loved going to the Baptist churches because they were lively and sang songs where everyone was jumping or shouting. I should say that the Methodist church was more structured politically where there was very little room for the Holy Spirit to manifest unlike the Baptist services where there were some expression of the Holy Spirit through man and was acknowledged by the Reverend; and he would say, "The Spirit of God is here." As I grew older, my hunger for the true God became a reality. Everyone can recall when they made that turn to Jesus Christ. They wondered, "Is there more, is this real, is there more to have of God?" I must admit that salvation through Jesus Christ was the start of my returning to God. I began attending a Baptist church. As a young adult, there appeared to be a drive in me to recommit my life to Christ. I wanted to know more of and about Him. As I would observe others and see them one way on Sunday and with another personality during the week, I just got disappointed. I began seeing that being a Christian member of the church really was another organization, not the kingdom of God. In reading the Bible, I saw these words:

> Be ye Holy for I am Holy. (1 Pet. 1:16b, KJV)

> Do not be conformed to this world (this age) [fashioned after and adapted to its external, superficial customs], but be transformed (changed) by the [entire] renewal of your mind [by its new ide- als and its new attitude], so that you may prove [for yourselves] what is the good and acceptable and perfect will of God, even the

things which is good and acceptable and perfect
[in His sight for you]. (Rom. 12:2, AMP)

But what I really saw were people trying to win a popu- larity contest, who you know, who liked you, wearing certain clothes and stylish hats. Boy, sometimes the women sitting in front of you, their hats blocked your view. I mean, is this book called the Bible another history book that had no real substance to live by? Are these words translated and written by Englishmen just to trap us? I recall looking at the TV series *Twilight Zone,* and some of the shows reflecting the future seem more realistic than the church.

One Saturday as I was rearranging my bedroom closet, I heard my name called "Theresa". I ignored it at first because I was home alone. Again, I heard "Theresa" this time it was louder. Looking puzzled I said yeah and then I thought girl you are hear- ing things and kept cleaning my closet out. Now I know, I should have said "Yes, Lord" and listen for Him to speak. As time passed, I kept seeking the truth. I knew I should be praying, so I did. I would be on my knees and would be crying and praying for the Lord to come, and sud- denly I would be on my knees and hands with my mouth forced to open. No sound, just opened wide, and my jaws locked. Well, this happened often. As I was reading more of the Bible, a desire for more of the Lord kept increasing. I became a leader in Southern Baptist Church as the president of the hospi- tality committee. I suggested to the committee to update the man- ual on how we served others. As a group, we fine-tuned ways to assist and serve the visiting churches. Our mission was to reflect a more excellent way to represent the kingdom of God. All parts of the hospitality committee, the food committee, hotel group, enter- tainment commit- tee, etc. and any other department that worked with visiting churches. I noticed that some members of the various com- mittees became more unified, desiring to reflect servanthood as the Lord demonstrated when he washed the disciples feet. One Friday in November of 1987, a sister from the church we attended called Southern Baptist. She was also a neighbor of mine, told me that the Lord told her to bring me to a women's fellowship. He told her that I wanted to know Him better. As a member of the women's group, she knew that this group was on fire for Christ. So I said okay, why not. I had nothing to lose. She came to pick me up later that evening, and off we went. She explained on the way that this group really loved Jesus, and that God wanted to let me see Him in a new light. Now, she was also my friend and the wife of one of the instructors at our church, who at that time was teaching from a book called *Dealing with the Devil*.[4] The class was every Sunday evening. We were learning the true mean- ing of being a Christian. Some of the material was about the Holy Spirit and His significates. This was intriguing to me.

When we arrived at the women's meeting, we were greeted with sincere expressions of love; at least, I picked that up. The room was full of sisters, some were new like myself. One of the members asked me was I baptized with the Holy Spirit and spoke with tongues.

I said, "Yeah, I have been baptized and emerged in water."

She politely said, "Nooo. I mean, baptized with the Holy Ghost and speak with tongues."

I said, "No. What is that?"

She said, "We'll show you after the meeting."

The fellowship was great. We sang songs, they prayed, calling it "praying in the spirit." I prayed in English along with a few others. The women were strong in the Word of God, speaking scriptures without the Bible. I recognized some or parts of the words spoken. At the end of the meet- ing, the question was asked by the leader: "Is there any one here that is not filled with the Holy Ghost and would like to experience the gift of the Holy Spirit?" I just stood there at first, and the lady that spoke with me earlier nudged me and whispered this is the opportunity that I was talking about your receiving the Holy Spirit. So I raised my hand and was brought to the back with others that wanted the baptism of the Holy Spirit. They explained what it entailed, and that I had to let my tongue loose and allow the Holy Spirit to speak through me.

---

4   *Dealing with the Devil* by C. S. Lovett.

They prayed with me; I felt a surge throughout my entire body, and when I let my tongue go, I spoke clearly, distinctly, and loudly. They said that I had been waiting to be released and I spoke as a mature born-again person, not a new beginner.

Wow, what an experience. I felt like my whole body was surged with the power of God, and now I was speaking a holy language. I now understood what the Lord was trying to get me to do during my previous prayer times. I was praying on the floor, on my knees and hands with my mouth grad- ually opened without a sound. I did not know I had to stop controlling my tongue and let the Holy Spirit speak through me. To stop allowing my flesh to control my spirit. I did not seize the moment in His presence for the lack of knowledge. How many of us do not seize the moment of His presence and embrace it? Just to know He is near. I was so excited and happy and felt love abundantly for anyone. When I went home that evening, I wanted to share with my husband, and I could hear the Holy Spirit tell me, "Not now, but the time will come. He will come to know Him in his season." The next day, I had changed my smallest bedroom to a prayer room. When I went to the prayer room, I prayed in tongues and with understanding. Oh, what fun it is to be in the pres- ence of God. I could see in the Spirit, hear in the Spirit. I was so excited about my new state of life that I made sure I spent time with the Lord and the Holy Spirit.

That evening I showed everyone in my family that this was the prayer room. My husband, my teenage daughter and the two little ones. So I took each child and had them to kneel and pray in that room, especially when they felt led by the Holy Spirit (they had been filled as well at ages five and six). (By the way, getting filled with the Holy Spirit and speaking with tongues has no age requirement.) I had a book in the room for them called *Prayers that Availeth Much for Children.* They were also free to use their own words that I am sure God heard and responded to their request. I, of course, used it early morning and late evenings. My husband also used his study. There is always something to continue praying for. The Bible says, "We ought to always pray without ceasing."

One night, while I was praying in tongues, I asked the Holy Spirit to reveal to me who I was praying for. In a vision, He let me see a small child between the age of three and four who was hurt and had fallen in a deep ditch in Africa. While I was praying, I saw him being rescued. Another occasion was when I was in a training session at my new church, which was an apostolic and prophetic church. That weekend began with training members how to understand their gifts and call- ings; our church had prophets from Christian International in Versailles, Indiana, that came to teach and impart to us. They instructed us on how to prophesy. They also explained the difference between the office of a prophet within the five-fold ministry and the gift of prophecy, which everyone can do with the Holy Spirit. That Saturday morning, the instructor had asked the class for three people to come up and prophesy to him. I raised my hand and proceeded to the front of the class. He said these simple words I will never forget. He had me say and pray: "Holy Spirit, reveal to me what you would have me to say to him." Immediately, as I looked at him, it was as if a giant book was laid before me as it opened. I told him that I see a sea of people in China. Then the page turned in Germany. Another page turned, and I said, "People in Africa and you were giving the Word of God. There will be signs, wonders and miracles, and I hear God saying soon."

His eyes teared and said, "That is what I have been praying for, and now God has confirmed my vision through you." He then said, "Praise God."

The Holy Spirit wants to be your friend, your standby, your advisor, and more. The Lord Jesus said in John 16:13– 14 (AMP),

> But when He, the Spirit of Truth (the Truth-giving Spirit) comes, He will guide you into all the Truth (the whole, full Truth). For He will not speak his own message (on His own authority); but He will tell whatever, He hears (from the Father; He will give the message that has been given to Him), and He will announce

and declare to you the things that are to come (that will happen in the future). He will honor and glorify Me, because He will take of (receive, draw upon) what is Mine and will reveal (declare, disclose, transmit) it to you.

We must believe and have faith that the Holy Spirit is sent to help us live here on earth and not be thinking of Him as a Ghost. Some still think that way because they do not have the correct information to understand who He really is or who He represents because they hear the name Ghost and think He is not real or is a Ghost. And we know that the noun ghost has been used by Satan to circumvent, kill, and destroy truth and change the meaning of ghost to be spooky, from hell, something man should stay away from with fear. The Bible tells the believer that:

> There is no fear in love, but perfect love casteth out fear, because fear hath tor- ment. He that feareth is not made perfect in love. (1 John 4:18, KJV)

It also says that the lack of knowledge causes one to perish.

> My people are destroyed for lack of knowledge; because you have rejected knowledge, I reject you from being a priest to me. (Hosea 4:6, ESV)

In the Book of John, Jesus tells the woman in Samaria at the well that

> The time is coming—indeed it's here now— when the true worshippers shall worship the Father in spirit and in truth: the Father is looking for those who will worship him that way. For God is Spirit, so those who worship him must worship in spirit and in truth. (John 4:23–24, NLT)

I was a member of the Southern Baptist Church with over 2,500 members. We understood that the Holy Ghost came upon the preacher, not the members. It was not taught as the next step after receiving Jesus Christ as your Lord and Savior, to receive the baptism of the Holy Ghost (Spirit). I was told it was for the holy rollers and of the devil. Because of that, it took time before I accepted the fact that I needed the Holy Spirit. Until my hunger and thirst for being closer to God drew me to others that were more knowledgeable than me, who had experienced and brought comfort from many myths, did I even feel comfortable with the idea. But I must say that if I had known what I know now, I would have accepted the Holy Spirit a long time ago. You feel like a new person capable of doing anything that will bring recognition and glorify God.

Well, as others may know from their experience, by my being baptized in the Holy Spirit, at my next hospital- ity committee announcement in front of the church that Sunday, my whole countenance had changed, and I spoke with joy down in my soul. The anointing was contagious, and people applauded the announcement. I was also the elev- enth-grade Sunday school teacher. When I went to teach the eleventh-grade Sunday school class, I wanted to shout from the house top that I have been filled with God's Spirit. What a blessing and honor to have the Spirit of God be literally inside of you. Wow.

As the love of God was shed aboard in my heart, I began to spread a greater love. My thoughts began to change; I wanted to love everyone, anyone, trees, bugs. The love of God in me was so strong that all I wanted to do was embrace everything. I could only see loving all. As I thought about love, it is the first fruit of the Spirit of God: love. So you know you have been filled with His Spirit for the presence of love is extraordinarily strong within you. My point of views changed with love as a priority. I suggested major changes with policy and mission statement modification and incor- porated a more kingdom view with the subcommittees in serving and wait- ing on people. I simply relied on the Holy Spirit to speak through me. That my body was dead in the spirit. That Jesus will send the

Holy Spirit to quicken my dead body and restore the life that I once knew with the Lord God and will quicken my spirit calling those things that be not as though they were. The same Spirit of Promise God used to quicken Abraham's dead body to impregnate Sarah is the same Holy Spirit that made me come alive (Rom. 4:17c). Guess what? He is the same Holy Spirit that raised Jesus out of the tomb. In my eleventh-grade Sunday School class, the students were at peace, cooperative, and they said there was something different about me. They enjoyed coming to the class even more so now. They began bringing their friends.

Well, a few weeks went by, and I was walking with the superintendent on the way to the Sunday school building. He asked why I was so happy. I, being still on high three weeks later, whispered to him in his ear, "I have been filled with the Holy Spirit." You would have thought I slapped him. He looked at me and said, "You have taught your last class and will not teach today." I was thinking that he was joking and laughed. As one of my husband's friends, I thought he would be happy for me. He was also the leader of the Male Chorus and part of the 4 All-star Male Chorus Group. When singing, they would shout and praise God. Surely, he would be excited the way they sang and praised God. Instead, he announced in the teachers' meeting room, prior to the Sunday school session, that I will not be teaching anymore and to let the substitute take my place that morning. I was shocked and hurt at the same time; I lost my thoughts and walked away, looking spaced as if I was a deer in the night looking at a car headlights. I gathered my youngest children who were five, six, fourteen and told my husband, the assistant superinten- dent, that the kids and I, we were leaving and went home. I was hurt because I loved working with the youth; they were hungry for the presence of God, loving the Lord.

I never went back to Southern Baptist. I felt rejected because they did not accept the Holy Spirit. If they did not want Him then they did not want me. A few weeks later, I prayed and asked the Holy Spirit where I should go. He directed me to visit the church that the leader of the women's group had prayed with me to receive the Holy Spirit called Word of Truth Ministries Church.

As time passed, my girls and I grew stronger in the Spirit. One of the things about the new church, they were on fire for Christ. We learned about the Holy Spirit and who He was, His significance in our lives, and that He would never leave or forsake us. I was asked to go with the leaders of the church to attend a conference called "How to Heal the Sick" with Charles and Frances Hunter in Columbus, Ohio. We learned how to lay hands on the sick and see immediate results. As leaders, we all came back to our groups and shared what we learned. The youth instructors shared with the chil- dren and youth. The children ages five and six and older were filled with the Holy Spirit and were so excited about their new friend called the Holy Spirit. They learned to pray and lay hands on the sick as well. This was so exciting; watching children in some cases do greater than the adults. They had no reason to doubt that God would flow through them. It was a fantastic anointed week. Years have passed, and the kids are adults doing other portions of ministry and confident that God still moves through them today.

My husband was a little puzzled about why I was not coming back to Southern Baptist Church with him. We usu- ally do things together and church is not any different. He was also one of the bus drivers for the church and one of the lead singers in the male chorus. He did not say much at first but later asked was I coming back. I said no. At that time, I never really said why I left, because the Holy Spirit had spo- ken before that my husband will come to know Him in time. Also because at that church they did not speak in tongues and the reverend forbid a class to teach about receiving the Holy Spirit. When he later asked why I was not coming to church. I simply told him that I found another church to come and visit. I also shared what happened with the Superintendent telling me I was not teaching anymore. I was hurt behind that and would not come back. It took a few months for him to come visit because of the soul ties he had with people and his responsibility as an inte- grous person. We were high school sweet hearts and trusted each other's lead and did not do too much separate from the other. He finally came. I knew he would be a little uncomfortable at the first visit because this congregation was singing from Integrity's CD's with the words on the screen and not a choir singing for us. Aside from the fact that this worship experience was all new to him it was a personal worship unto God and we did not have a male chorus he could join. He eventually joined after having more visits and teaching on the gospel that brought clarity enough where he understood what else outside of salvation the Lord Jesus provided for us on the cross. Which included His followers to receive the Holy Spirit, the comforter, stand by, your personal consultant that can keep you from falling.

It was almost a year before my husband surrendered to accepting the Holy Spirit. I saw him trying to hold onto religion. He struggled at first, as most people do. However, being among born again spirit filled saints and attending conferences where the Holy Spirit was in charge. My hus- band's heart was willing to accept the Holy Spirit. Months later we went to the School of the Holy Spirit at Christian International in Versailles, Indiana. When the worship was over and the attendees broke up into groups for a prophetic word, my husband hesitated at first but the Holy Spirit urged him to come over. As they prophesied over us the word was impactive to both of us. The Lord brought comfort in His word especially to my husband on God's next moves in His life. Who he was in Christ and that God calls him his Son. That He loved him and was a man after his own heart. A prayer warrior and that there are great things in store for him.

The word came from an individual he did not know so he knew it was from God and his prayers answered. My teens were given words of direction and confirmation on their future because of their obedience. My husband was in awe. We all were highly blessed. Later that month he accepted the Holy Spirit and began growing in leaps and bounds. He never knew his biological father to hear that God loved him and called him son. Encouraged him to become a valiant man of God. As time passed, if I was not ready to leave for church and he felt that he would not be on time, he would let me know he was leaving and I would have to drive myself. The Holy Spirit drew us closer than we were in the natural. We prayed together, cried when things went wrong according to what we believed in the Bible. We sought the Lord God separately and in unity. We became a three-fold cord and cleaved tighter to each other. Up until the Lord God called Him home January 15, 2006. We were forever grateful for the times we spent spiritually unified. It is by the Holy Spirit that I am now ready to share this season that included my high school sweetheart and later my husband. Our unity with God made all the difference in our marriage and life. There were some challenges but God knows our time on earth. And thank God my husband is in heaven. I will see him again. I am blessed because my family and I have received God's door for our eternal destiny. I pray that you will also accept the work of the cross that opened Destiny's Door, the Holy Spirit.

REVERSING MY WILL

In the spring of 1988, I had a challenge with the infirmity called Lupus. Because of what I had learned from my leaders and training from Christian International deliverance ses- sions, I asked my mother did she recall if any other family member had this infirmity. She did not know of anyone in our family that had encountered this disease; I was the first. According to the training, I learned that curses, diseases, negative characteristics are transferred through families as a Spirit of Inheritance and generational curses they say passed down through families by the programming of the DNA. In Exodus 20:5 (KJV), God says, "I the Lord thy God am a jealous God, visiting the iniquity of the fathers upon the children unto the third and fourth generation of them that hate me."

This scripture in the bible lets us know that we are dealing with inter-generational spirits, a familiar spirit of ill- nesses. Diabetes, heart issues, high or low blood pressure and the latest, cancer.

Families accept these faults and enforce them by saying, "My mother had it, my uncle used to do it, all of my family had diabe- tes." This will go on, as the Bible says, from one generation to the next, to the third and fourth generations. It will continue until a member takes the authority given by God to end that curse/disease/sin from continuing to travel through the family. We as born-again, spirit-filled, Bible- reading Christians, have been given the authority to end the familiar spirit from transferring to you and those after you. Since I did not have a specific family curse, to track or trace in my generational bloodline I had nothing to bind or uproot, I relied totally on the Holy Spirit to help me end this infirmity (disease) and not let it pass on to another family member breaking the curse. You see sickness is not ordered by God. What Jesus did on the cross receiving the stripes ends it all. We tend to forget what benefits came because of the cross.

As I shared earlier, regarding my challenge, my zealous- ness to believe without faith, I had just went in for a typi- cal physical checkup, and my doctor, who was in internal medicine named Dr. Mathew, diagnosed that I had lupus. I frowned and denounced his words openly. "I am afraid that you are wrong." But he insisted because of my blood test. When I left the checkup, in my eagerness to be healed, I became angry and thought, "How dare the devil crossing the bloodline and touching me! Who does he think he is?" As a new born-again Christian, I thought that I was untouchable. I would bind and rebuke anything I thought was associated with the devil; this means war. As one of the leaders in my church and a workman rightly dividing the word of truth. I understood one of the precepts in the Bible regarding leader's is that no one is an island. Our responsibility as leaders is to communicate in spirit and in truth according to the Word of God which counteracts the plot of Satan.

"Where no counsel is, the people fall: but in the multitude of counsellors there is **safety***" (Prov. 11:14, KJV).*

Another translation *says: When there is no guidance a nation falls, but there is success in the abundance of counselors. (NET)*

So I called upon my elders in the church, as the Word instructs us in James 5:14–15 (KJV):

> Is any sick among you? Let him call for the
> elders of the church, let them pray over him,
> anointing him with oil in the name of the Lord:

And the prayer of the faith shall save the sick,
and the Lord shall raise him up, and if he
committed sines, they shall be forgiven him.

Confess your faults one to another, and prey one for another
that ye may be healed. The effectual fervent prayer of a righteous
man availeth much (James 5:16, KJV).

Late that afternoon, they came to my house, prayed for me,
and anointed my head. The three of us touched and agreed that
I was already healed. The Word of God tells us that when two or
three are gathered in His name that He is in the midst of us. We
were in like minds and one accord. By faith we knew I was healed.
Well, in the next few days, whatever I ate came right on through.
I thought I had the bug and simply detoxing. To me, I was losing
weight, so I ate what I wanted. No matter what I ate, nothing
stayed in my body. The following week, when I got up to dress for
work, I was looking in the mirror to wash my face when I noticed
on my cheeks I had what appeared to be third-degree burns. I
started thinking about the night cream I used or something I ate
the night before. Reluctantly, I called the doctor, and he said, "It
was the lupus I told you about."

Well, if that diagnosis was not enough, in the following days and
weeks, other changes started occurring. My hair was thinning; various
spots were appearing all over my body, not to mention the fact that
my body did not digest foods prop- erly and still losing weight. I am
sure all of us who love food would enjoy the fact that I could eat anything, and it would not turn into the grudged fat I hated. I was losing
weight without a diet or lack of food. Now, that part was good but not
under these circumstances. I became angry again.

While in prayer with the Holy Spirit, He reminded me about
Job. He let me know that I will go through like Job. He told me,
"For this is not unto death." He brought comfort to me, and I
began to relax. When I went to the doctor a few days later, he
said I had two accounts of lupus. I had the but- terfly on my face,
and my entire immune system was break- ing down rapidly. He
ordered steroids and liquid chemo. His office contacted me to let

me know that a nurse was coming to give me the chemo. The next week, a nurse came to my home, set up the equipment to give me seven hundred milli- grams of liquid chemo.

Now, I was some young born-again sister in the Lord and would bind and lose any demon or human that crossed my path that I thought was out of order. I am sure those of you who have experienced the initial infilling of the Holy Spirit can attest to my attitude and boldness. Before the nurse came to administer the treatment, I said to the Lord that I know He died on the cross and took a stripe on His body for my healing, and I was not taking the medication or the chemo. Then I heard with a loud voice: "Do not tempt the Lord thy God." Well, He did not have to say anything else. I decided to take the chemo. Before the nurse came, I prayed that the medication would have a reverse effect and not do what man believed, that my flesh would repeal the treatment, and God's healing power would take place, so He gets the glory. Needless to say, I took the medication of steroids and the one chemo injection. No problem. After a few days passed, I then started looking like a leopard. Things were happening so fast I did not know what to do. Along with my losing weight, my teeth started loosening in my gums; my vision was dimming; my feeling in my hands were all gone to where I could not feel any temperature; my sense of touch was gone. I thank God that I knew when things on the stove were hot or when I turned on the water in the bathroom. I understood which way the knob should be turned for cold or hot or which knife was sharp and how to use it when cooking. Next, I started losing my hair. All my five senses decreased daily. I really felt like Job. I thought about how Job believed God and stayed focus. I also started thinking about what the Holy Spirit told me about: this is not unto death. When I looked in the mir- ror, unbelief tried to set in my thoughts. While my mind was still renewing as I was reading the bible, my flesh was trying to keep me in doubt. What I was seeing was my body destroying itself. I wanted to panic, but I couldn't and main- tained my faith. I began reciting scriptures while the Holy Spirit was bringing them to my remembrance. I had faith in God and was determined I was healed and believed God for His word which said:

> That Jesus was wounded for (my) our transgressions. He was bruised for our guilt and iniquities; the chastisement [needful to obtain] peace and well-be- ing for us was upon Him, and with the stripes [that wounded] Him *we are healed and made whole*. (Isa. 53:5–6, AMP)

> Who, when he was reviled, reviled not again; when he suffered, he threatened not; but committed himself to him that judgeth righteously: Who his own self bare our sins in his own body on the tree, that we, being dead to sins, should live unto righteousness: by whose stripes ye were healed. (1 Pet. 2:23–24, KJV)

Another translation says it this way:

> When he was maligned, he did not answer back; when he suffered, he threat- ened no retaliation, but committed him- self to God who judges justly. 24 He himself bore our sins in his body on the tree, that we may cease from sinning and live for righteousness. By his wounds you were healed. (1 Pet. 2:23–24, NET)

The elders in my church emphasized that reading the word is our survival kit. In my reading I recalled an event in the bible where this lady had an issue of blood for twelve years. Now I remembered the doctor telling me that the he diag- nosed the Lupus because of my blood test. This lady had gone to doctors, spent all her money for help and instead of them helping her, it got worse. When she heard of Jesus healing peo- ple and he was in town. She pushed her way to him thinking that if she could only touch his garment that she would be made whole. Her faith was so strong that it drew from Jesus anointing to her spirit and He wanted to know who touched Him in the middle of a crowd of people. Somebody with faith touched him, not with doubt or apprehension. He did not do anything directly to them. She knew in her heart that all she needed was to get in His presence and receive what Jesus offered freely because of who He is. The disciples said how can we know with all these people around you. When she fell at His feet and told Him the truth. Jesus said to her that her faith had made her whole (Mark 5:25–34, KJV). Her faith became so strong in her that it pulled from the Lord and released heal- ing. She just knew that if she could just get any part of Jesus she would be healed. I kept reading that scripture and com- manding myself to have faith like her. Have faith that the word of God will heal you. Have faith in the Lord God. Jesus is the Word that was made flesh and dwelt among us, (and we beheld his glory, the glory as of the only begotten of the Father) full of grace and truth (John 1:14, KJV). I learned that Faith is a force that takes hold of the answer God has already provided for us. He gives divine health to all that believes in Jesus Christ work on the cross making it available to us immedi- ately. I did not have to do anything but stay in faith.

I clung onto the word of God declaring and decreeing that I was already healed. When I looked in the mirror my joints were aching with rheumatoid athritis, I thought about throwing in the towel. I looked like the actor in the original version of the movie *The Phantom of the Opera* with just a few strands of hair on my head. The Holy Spirit, thank God for Him, reminded me of the book of Job and how he was tempted of the devil by permission only. So at that time, I felt honored that God had that kind of confidence in me to be able to go through this season of my life. This gave me increased faith that Jesus was carrying me through. I do not know what I would have done without the Holy Spirit guiding and leading me.

> Now Faith is the assurance (the confir- mation,
> the title deed) of the things (we) hope for being
> the proof of things (we) do not see and the
> conviction of their reality (faith perceiving as

real fact what is not revealed to the senses). (Heb. 11:1, AMP)

Early the following week I got a call from one of my intercessory partners who was very secure in the Spirit of God. She told me that the Holy Spirit told her to call me and tell me to fast for three days. The next day I asked the Holy Spirit how should I fast with medication? He told me to do it with milk and honey only and to take my medica- tion. My mother was a little upset with me, being a nurse, she wanted me to eat something with the steroid. But I was fasting as instructed by the Holy Spirit who would keep me in this called fast. Fasting throughout the word of God. Is to abstain from food like the Lord Jesus or Ester demonstrated. Especially when you are called to a fast. God will sustain the body He created. So I did the three days along with contin- ually praying. My apostle's wife gave me a copy of a prayer she said will help me pull through. She said that I was a tena- cious minister, and it would help me pull through. At that time, it was called "The Overcomer's Confession." It was full of scriptures that helped me stay focused on who I was in Christ, and it became a part of my daily bread, still today.

Father,

Lead me not into temptation but deliver me from evil. (Matt. 6:13)

I will not let the devil take advantage of me and sift me as wheat. (Luke 22:31).

I trust in You alone to provide an escape from all temptations. (1 Cor. 10:13).

My strength comes from the power of the Lord as I clothe myself with

The whole armor of God. (Eph. 6:11–17)

The Belt of Truth—I will fill my innermost being with Your truth.

The Breastplate of Righteousness— Your righteousness will protect my heart, for out of it flows the issues of life.

My feet are shoed with the prepara- tion of the Gospel of Peace—It gives me the stability to proclaim the Gospel (that Jesus died, was buried, and rose again) to those in my path today.

The Shield of Faith—Although it does not keep me out of the battle but will protect me in it quenching every fiery dart toward me, both offensively and defensively.

The Helmet of Salvation—I shelter my mind from Satan's attacks of doubt, depression, suppression, oppression, and discouragement with the helmet of salvation.

The Sword of the Spirit—I will use Your sword, which is the Word of God, which defeats the devil, not my words.

The Garment of Praise for the Spirit of Heaviness—I make the decision to praise You, oh God in all things today, no matter what it looks like.

I am more than a conqueror through the blood of Jesus.

I am redeemed out of the hand of Satan (Ps. 107:2).

I am cleansed continually from all sins (1 John 1:7).

I am justified and made righteous through faith (Rom. 5:6).

I am sanctified, made holy and set apart to God (Heb. 13:12).

I am free from the fear of hell, the grave and death (Rom. 8:2, Gal. 3:13).

I am healed of all sickness and disease (Isa. 53:5. 1 Pet. 2:24) and guilt (Rom. 8:1).

I am forgiven (Eph. 1:7) and all my sins are forgiven (Isa. 43:25).

I know Satan is a bluff, a liar and a thief (John 8:44, 10:10).

Satan has no place, no power and no unsettled claims against me (Rom. 8:33–34).

On the Cross the battle was won and Satan was made a public display (Col. 2:14–15)

I have authority over all the powers of darkness and I fear nothing (Luke 10:19).

I have the same power in me that rose Jesus from the dead (Rom. 8:11).

Jesus and His power are the same yester- day, today and forever (Heb. 13:8).

I can do all things through Christ who strengthens me (Phil. 4:13).

I overcome the devil by the Blood of the Lamb and the word of my testimony and I love not my life unto death (Rev. 12:11).

Father,

I ask that every carnal prayer, every neg- ative statement and every curse spoken against me or by me be broken today in the name of Jesus. I ask that the harvest of negative seeds I have sown be cut off, and the harvest of positive seeds be has- tened, for I know that as I have sown so shall I reap. (Gal. 6:7–8).

Fill me with the knowledge of Your will today in all spiritual wisdom and under- standing so I may walk in a manner wor- thy of You, to please You, bearing good fruit and increasing in the knowledge of You. (Col. 1:9–10)

This prayer and Psalm 91 were building my faith to stay focus on the Word of God even today. Not only the prayer but because Jesus said we are overcomers by the Blood of the Lamb and the words of our testimonies (Rev. 12:11, KJV). Jesus has made us victorious.

While I was drastically changing in appearance, one night I had a dream that I was on one side of a fire that went across the front of me about 10 feet away from me and six feet high, but it was not hot. The fire was amber and shin- ning gold in color. As I was looking through the fire, I saw Jesus with His arms opened and His hands beckoning me to come through the fire. Like Peter walked on the water, I got up and came through the fire that I believed represented the lupus. I saw the stripe on His body that represented diseases associated with the immune system breaking down. It was as if the disease left me and was illuminating on Jesus body. He showed me the stripe He took for Lupus was back on Him and the Lupus was released from me. I had more faith espe- cially once I saw and understood what He did for me so vividly. I felt so free. Some would say at ease or feeling light as the burden was lifted and I no longer had to carry Lupus. I still tear up when I think about it. The weird thing about it is, it no longer mattered about what my natural eye would see or what my body felt. I had faith in God. Hallelujah! When I woke up, I felt stronger, I had hope, and my faith increased to great faith. At the moment, I got out of my sleep for some reason I knew that I was healed. Nothing could make me feel any different. My confidence became stronger, my faith enlarged, I got very strong. I even felt completely healed because of the words spoken to me by the Holy Spirit, and the Lord beckoned me to come through the fire of lupus. I understood that I did not have to wear lupus anymore and that Jesus took one of the thirty-nine stripes that represented lupus for me to be healed with divine health while here on earth. I have faith in my spirit enough that I believed, at that moment, the destructive curse on my body stopped and reversed to restore.

Later that week while I was in my bed room, I had a vision. I saw one of my sisters in Christ coming about four blocks way. The Holy Spirit told me that she was coming to visit and would not stay. When she arrived my mother called me to come up stairs that I have a guest. Now mind you I only had a few strands of hair. My face still had the burn marks on my cheeks and had lost weight. Wearing my robe I came around the corner. She said in shock and fear, "Oh, I came to give you some flowers" and stuttered as she turned and started down the Forer steps and said that she had to leave I pray you will get better. She then left out the door. I had so much anointing on me that it brought fear on her. Now she was one of the talking sisters that can talk your head off. But she left.

I did not realize that because of my time with the Lord, reading the Bible and worshipping Him had changed my presence. I really was not trying to scare her, for we had been friends for a few years since the women's fellowship, where I received the Holy Spirit. So I was shocked. But later I under- stood that the Holy Spirit increases in us when a person around us is in need for the presence of God to heal, answer prayers, or just being with Him. She left so fast out of fear; she missed the opportunity to be in the presence of God. She had a need, and He was present to meet that need. How did I know it? Because the Holy Spirit increase and filled me letting me know that God wanted to restore and repair this vessel. I would not have known it without Him in the natu- ral state. Even today the Holy Spirit of Almighty God wants to reach his children and restore, repair, and renew all even though we go astray like some of the disciples—namely, Peter and Doubting Thomas. For the Lord God desires that none be lost whoever accepts Jesus Christ as their Savior. For the Lord has prayed for His followers in the book of John 17:12 and 18:9 (KJV).

> While I was with them in the world, I kept them in thy name; those that thou gavest me I have kept, and none of them is lost, but the son of perdition, that the scripture might be fulfilled.

NET translation of John 18:9 confirms 17 and says:

> He said this to fulfill the word he had spoken, "I have not lost a single one of those whom you gave me."

Keep in mind that Jesus is demonstrating to the disci- ples/apostles what the kingdom of God is like. Yet it also is the responsibility of all followers as ambassadors of Christ— to help restore another follower of Christ.

Our will is always in the survival state for oneself. But when we study the Word of God and allow the Holy Spirit to reverse our will to God's will, we win eternal life.

SUBMITTING TO THE HOLY SPIRIT

He called a little child and had him stand among them. And He said: "I tell you the truth, unless you change and become like little children, you will never enter the kingdom of heaven. Therefore, whoever humbles himself like this child is the greatest in the kingdom of heaven. And whoever welcome a little child like this in my name, welcomes me.

—Matthew 18:2–5 (NLT)

During my challenge with lupus, the Holy Spirit began waking me up daily at 2:30 a.m. and drew me to the prayer room. He helped me read the Word of God. Why? Because the Word of God is medication to my flesh.

My son, give attention to my words; Submit to my sayings. Let them not depart from your sight; Keep them in the center of your heart; For they

[are] life to those that find them, healing and
health to all their flesh. (Prov. 4:20–22, AMP)

At 2:30 a.m. my eyes would gently open and I would get out
of bed and go to the prayer room. The Holy Spirit and I fellow-
shipped through the Bible. It began to feel like I was replacing
my condition. For lack of words I was watching my flesh yield to
the Word which is the Lord. I saw my body gradually restore as I
learned to submit and receive what the Lord provided as a benefit
from the cross. I wanted to know more about Jesus, understand
what He did for me as a cove- nant daughter of Zion. I chose like
Mary Magdalene to stay at Jesus feet. I loved having this time
with the Holy Spirit of God. It was all I was living for. I wanted
the Lord God to get all the glory. My body was so light. I was not
really paying attention with the changes being made in me, I was
not con- cerned since I turned my life over to God. I no longer
wanted to be me but what God planned and purposed for me. The
Holy Spirit was constantly repairing and restoring my spirit (me)
and the earthen vessel (body) with the Word of God.

"No one sews a patch of unshrunk clothe on an
old garment, Because the patch will pull away
from the garment and the tear will be worse.
And no one pours new wine into old wineskins;
otherwise the skins burst and the wine is spilled
out and the skins are destroyed. Instead, they
put new wine into new wineskins and both are
preserved. (Matt. 9:16–17, NET)

One morning after worshipping the Lord, the Holy Spirit
was stronger in me. My renewed spirit was synchro- nized with the
Holy Spirit and my senses changed. The spir- it-filled portion of
me was receiving the new wine which is the word of God. And the
word of God was restoring my body. I suddenly began to absorb
the Word of God through my spirit instead of reading the Word of
God with my nat- ural eyes. I began scanning the Bible instead of

reading with such rapid speed. I was flipping the pages, looking up and down the pages of the Bible in lieu of reading a page from left to right, line upon line. My flesh absorbed the Word like a sponge soaking in the words of life as medication but with the power of God. As the Creator of all of us, He knew what to do. My faith became greater and greater, stronger and stron- ger. During my prayer time with the Holy Spirit, I could hear when my husband would get up out of bed and begin dress- ing for work all the way in the back of the house. I have a tri-level home and the prayer room Is in the front over the two-car garage. Our bedroom is in the new addition in the lower back of the house. He was such a support, not knowing what was going on, but he respected my leaving the room and my many hours in prayer and never questioned me. He saw the changes and was happy that his wife was being restored.

My prayer time with the Holy Spirit developed a rela- tionship of a very close friend. My time with Him became a worship. One morning while worshipping the Father, I began to dance, and He picked me up. My feet were off the carpet, and we danced around the room. I felt so connected with Him; He was the best dancing partner I had ever had. When we were done with worshipping God Almighty, He sat me down and we read more Word, turning pages and healing my flesh through my spirit. This became a daily appointment. It is hard to explain such gentle power with human words. Or watching your body repairing itself from a humbling state, like Job or Hezekiah, with your body changing to perfection quickly without chemo or strong medications. Each time I came for examination, my doctor would be amazed. He had to always decrease my medication; he thought I would need to reluctantly remove it. He had an excuse to keep .5 mil- ligram for four weeks because the steroids had to gradually taper down to avoid side effects. He felt I was in remission.

My response to him was that I was healed and did not need the one steroid.

Now, we all are familiar with our body being first, fol- lowed by the soul, and last our spirit. Well, my spirit became stronger and stronger until I experienced the spirit transform- ing my fleshly ways as He was killing me softly. The Word was taking over my flesh. I felt the anointing like a full body scuba diver's suit without the footwear or oxygen tank. I was lining up in kingdom order. My mind had transformed completely with the Word of God, and my spirit became stronger than my flesh. My spirit became so much stronger merging with the Holy Spirit until my soul willfully and completely surrendered to Him. When I got out of bed, I would kneel and bow my head to God. Then I would get up and go to the prayer room. My personality changed; I was dying to myself. The apostle Paul said, "I die daily." As I continued to worship God and embrace Him like never before, my body who I controlled all of my life now bowed down to the Holy One of Israel, follow- ing His lead. My mind and thoughts were only for the lost, captive, and the spiritually dead. My flesh could not get into the Holy Place, but my spirit accompanied and readied by the Holy Spirit could. By the end of the week, I had absorbed the entire Bible. By the begin- ning of the next week, I began to feel my body as a costume over my spirit. I could look out through my eye sockets as though I was wearing a full-face mask. I could hear my self breathing behind the mask. The firstborn Theresa was dead. I no longer had control of me. It was then that I understood the Word when it said,

> Ye are of God, little children, and have overcome them: Because greater is he that is in you, than he that is in the world. (1 John 4:4, KJV)

> Hereby know we that we dwell in him, and he in us, because he hath given us of his Spirit. And we have seen and do tes- tify that the Father sent the Son to be the Saviour of the world. (1 John 4:13–14, KJV)

Over the time, I had lost so much weight that my dress size decreased from eighteen to zero, which was the opposite of steroid reaction to the human body. I then understood that this earth suit (my body) was only a covering for the real me which was sent from heaven to earth through the womb of my mother, which also meant that as a spirit-filled creation, my purpose is centered on bringing the kingdom of God to the earth. And nothing else, by any means, mat- tered. I now understood that faith is a force that overcomes the works of the flesh and it is not a work that I could do. In the natural life I was studying the word like I did for my classes in school. Or memorizing the laws and trying not to do what was wrong at work and follow company policy. Although I knew the organization's constitution/laws. I was just knowing them with head knowledge not applying them spiritually. The Bible's content is to change a person into another way of living confidentially, holy with a pure heart and replace my character. As the Lord had said to many in the bible that their faith had made them whole as they were challenged with a disease or circumstance. I believe all of the bible. Each portion of the bible enhances the development of a believer. That is why we must study the Word of God on our own. To know the truth that makes us free. So, my faith in the word of God helped my will to overcome my earthly habit of self-control and what I taught myself to rely on. As the Word changed my thoughts, I believed the report of the Lord. I had faith in the Word of God and would not compro- mise His word for man's words. I knew that the knowledge of the Word applied with faith would make me a victor. Jesus already provided my healing. Like the woman that had the issue of blood and knew when she touched His garment that she would be made whole. I drew the virtue out of the Word and held onto it like a bulldog holds onto the person he has gripped with his jaws.

As my body became fully restored, I was asked by the Pastor's wife to bring my witness to a women's conference. When I shared many were restored. I was able to be used of God unconditionally. Namely, I could see in the spirit, hear sounds from heaven and hear the voice of the Holy Spirit as clearly as if He was sitting right next to me. I found that once the Lord's provision is accepted by faith, the total restoration will manifest. It does not take years.

Ask the Lord Jesus to help you further understand what I am about to say. By now you should realize that today it is about whose kingdom you are standing with. It is either the Kingdom of God or the World of Satan.

I beseech you, saints of God, to surrender yourself to God, and if you have not already, accept the Holy Spirit today. Don't question or doubt God as Thomas did. He had to see the nail punctures in Jesus's hand and in His side before he could believe Jesus had risen and was alive. Even though Jesus was standing in front of him Blessed is he who has not seen and yet believe. You have had enough informa- tion, demonstration, and direction in this book. My prayer to you is this: "Lord God, help them to hear Your word and surrender all they have to You for Your Glory."

For those who have not had the infilling of the Holy Spirit with the gift and evidence of speaking in tongues, remember: you have to let your tongue loose and allow the Holy Spirit to speak through you. Relax and let it rip. Pray the following:

> Father, forgive me for all my sins (Listen for He will tell you and say what you hear). I repent of those sins, I ask for Your forgiveness. For You have said in the Word that if I shall confess with my mouth, the Lord Jesus, and believe in my heart that God has raised Him for the dead, I shall be saved. For with the heart man believes unto righteousness, and with my mouth, confession is made unto salvation. (Pause) and say, "Jesus, fill me, Lord, with the Holy Spirit as You prom- ised in Your word that out of your belly shall flow rivers of living water." (Pause and wait for the overflow.)

You will feel as if your mouth wants to move without you (a little awkward). Relax and let it happen. Let the new words come out of your mouth by the Holy Spirit of God which will be an unlearned language. A wonderful surge of life will go through your entire body, who is the Holy Spirit, and your body now becomes born again in the Spirit. You now have the heavenly language that you can pray to the Father without the devil being able to interfere with what you want from the Lord and what God has planned spe- cifically for you. You have now begun "to kill the firstborn" and the elder (who is you born of your mother and earthly father) and had years on the earth prior to you being filled. You now have the Holy Spirit giving you a new birthday in the spirit. Since you have accepted the Holy Spirit, your spiritual birth with Him will now begin renewing you back into kingdom of God, and the younger you will start ruling the one born of the flesh, a.k.a the elder, the firstborn. Now, the new you need only to study the Bible (<u>B</u>asic <u>I</u>nstructions <u>B</u>efore <u>L</u>eaving <u>E</u>arth: BIBLE) in the King James version preferably. The King James Bible translated by Englishmen from the Hebrews & Greek Bibles will help you to know Jesus as the Holy Spirit first wrote the Word of God, as well as your kingdom citizenship authority. Do not forget that you have submitted to God and the work of the cross from Jesus. Your submission now protects you from the enemy death, hell, and the grave and registers you in heaven. God's word tells all to study to show thyself approved unto God, a workman that needeth not be ashamed, rightly dividing the word of truth. But shun profane and vain babblings: for they will increase unto more ungodliness (2 Tim. 2:15–16, KJV). God the Father is so sure of what He has promised us that he made a sealed promise with the Holy Spirit. Not only that, the Lord God makes a covenant with us through the blood shed by Jesus Christ our Saviour. Because God is a covenant keeping God the covenant can only be broken by you. Choose the right covenant. There are all kinds of cove- nants and vows but God's new and better covenant through Jesus Christ provides righteousness and right standing with Him. Many have not cho- sen to select all that God provided for us to return back to Him under the new covenant. Most still choose to live in confusion, doubt, and fear and cling to the old covenant or Laws and grasp- ing at the threads of grace and mercy. Don't live that way! Begin today and accept the Holy Spirit who will guide you into all truth and help you to understand the bible. Remember, it was the Holy

Spirit that inspired the writers and the interpreters to put the <u>B</u>asic Instructions <u>B</u>efore <u>L</u>eaving <u>E</u>arth in writing for you and for me.

> It is not that we think we are qualified to do anything on our own. Our qualifica- tion comes from God. He has enabled us to be ministers of his new covenant… If the old way, which brings condemnation, was glorious, how much more glorious is the new way, which makes us right with God! (1 Cor. 3:5–6, 9 NLT)

hallelujah! I once heard a well know anointed woman of God, named Kathryn Kuhlman say in one of her messages "that we must cooperate with the Holy Spirit and that we do not have to understand just obey." Give Him praise and thank Him for the kingdom of God is with and in you now.

Another book that God has inspired me to write that will strengthen your walk in the Spirit is *Vessels of Silver and Gold* coming soon.

ABOUT THE AUTHOR

Having gone through a life-threatening disease, many know as Lupus, this kind of Lupus caused her body to begin destroy- ing itself. It effected, her entire nervous system and tried to terminate her life. Theresa T. Stark will tell anyone that it was Jesus Christ that paved the way for her to be victorious and an overcomer. As an ordained prophetic minister, God has blessed her to print her combined victory with healing that is because of Jesus's Christ work of the cross. It still sustains her today and never been in remission. Glory!

"Be steadfast and immovable" is the heart of this author. Wanting all to become vessels of the Kingdom of God. As a teacher with groups from teens to adults rightly dividing the word of Truth, she has been greatly respected and loved by many. Those that have seen her life know her life to be more walking the walk than talking the talk. Being a pro- phetic ordained minister of God as well as an intercessor of the Kingdom of God, she desires as the Father that all men be saved and come into the knowledge of the truth, reaching their fullness in life as God planned. Her passion for others to become a spiritual being has been with numerous chal- lenges and years to put this book into script. She found that her desire to obey God rather than herself is a greater reward. With the help of the Holy Spirit while studying the Word of God, she is now able to share this dynamic walk in a book.

Theresa is an unknown to be known in this season to glorify God.